PENGUIN BOOKS

OF LIFE AND LIES

Catherine Dellosa plays video games for a living, reads comics for inspiration, and writes fiction because she's in love with words. She lives in Manila, Philippines with her husband, whose ideas fuel the fire in her writing.

Her Young Adult fantasy novel, *Of Myths And Men,* has been published by Penguin Random House SEA and is her love letter to gamer geeks, mythological creatures, aliens, and epic quests to save the world. *Of Life And Lies* is the second book in the trilogy. She is currently working on a few more projects up her sleeve.

She has also penned *The Choices We Made (And Those We Didn't)* published by BRUMultiverse, as well as *Raya and Grayson's Guide to Saving the World* and *The Bookshop Back Home* as part of #romanceclass—a community of Filipino authors who are equally in love with words too.

When she's not lost in the land of make-believe, she works as a games journalist for one of the biggest mobile gaming media outlets in the UK. She one day hopes to soar the skies as a superhero, but for now, she strongly believes in saving lives through her works in fiction. Check out her books at bit.ly/catherinedellosabooks, or follow her on FB/IG/Twitter at @thenoobwife.

Praise for *Of Life and Lies*

'Right on the heels of the pacey *Of Myths and Men* is its sequel featuring the gutsy protagonist Ava and the endearing ensemble cast of supernatural characters—from elves to *manananggals* to manticores to dragon-horses. With an inventive blend of folklore and fantasy, a twisty action-packed plot that keeps you on the edge of your seat, and a fun host of supporting characters, this is one affirmative book for gamers and RPG-lovers!'

—Joyce Chua, author of *Land of Sand and Song*

'Masterful storytelling and world building. Action-packed and a page-turner.'

—Eva Wong Nava,
author of magic realism
YA novel, *The House of Little Sisters*

'Catherine raises the stakes in this sequel and spins a fun and gripping tale that'll have you on the edge of your seat as her protagonist, Ava, tries to save the world from colonizing aliens together with an ensemble cast of mythical creatures from both Western and Asian folklore.'

—Leslie W., author of *The Night of Legends* trilogy

Of Life and Lies

Catherine Dellosa

PENGUIN BOOKS

An imprint of Penguin Random House

PENGUIN BOOKS

USA | Canada | UK | Ireland | Australia
New Zealand | India | South Africa | China | Southeast Asia

Penguin Books is part of the Penguin Random House group of companies
whose addresses can be found at global.penguinrandomhouse.com

Published by Penguin Random House SEA Pvt. Ltd
9, Changi South Street 3, Level 08-01,
Singapore 486361

First published in Penguin Books by Penguin Random House SEA 2023
Copyright © Catherine Dellosa 2023

ISBN 9789815127096

Typeset in Garamond by MAP Systems, Bangalore, India

www.penguin.sg

Contents

Prologue   vii

1. New Game Plus   1
2. Damage Per Second   6
3. Timed Challenge   16
4. Escort Quest   30
5. Player Two   41
6. PvP   52
7. Weapons Upgrade   63
8. Farming   74
9. World Map   90
10. Quality-Of-Life Update   99
11. Secret Character   112
12. Nerfed   125
13. X Joins Your Party   136
14. Extra Life   152
15. Continue?   164

Acknowledgements   169

Prologue

It was all fun and games until the evil aliens came.

Sorry—I should probably start this like a real letter. Didn't we always say we wanted to write actual, physical letters to each other like old-school BFFs? Now's as good a time as any, I guess. It's the end of the world, after all.

So.

Dear Cassie,

How've you been? I know we haven't spoken to each other since that day I called you about this fake retreat—you obviously know by now that I made it all up; I'm sorry—but I want you to know I still think of you, and I feel terrible about lying to you. I should've told you everything that was happening to me, and this letter may be a poor excuse, but I'm writing this now, and even though I'll never get to send it, never get to see you or talk to you, I'd still like to try. I'd still like to make up for all the things I never got to say, so.

It was all fun and games until the evil aliens came.

If I sound like I'm about to bore you with another one of my video games' stories, I'm sorry. But I swear it's all true. That retreat I told you I went to in the woods? It was actually a secret camp filled with mythological creatures—or, at least, what we believe to be mythological creatures. In reality, they're aliens—the real E.T. stuff—and they've been hiding out here on Earth like refugees.

Remember the ghosts I used to see when we were kids? The full-on dead people hanging around in my house? Turns out they're not really spirits of humans who've passed on—they're called the Pure, and they were driven out from their home planet by another alien race called the Hostiles (derivative, isn't it?). The catch is that the Pure can't live in the Earth's atmosphere for too long, so they do this thing called the Binding, where they Bind with human corpses to survive.

The thing is, they never do know how one Binding might turn out—some of them morph into more humanoid forms while others turn into animal hybrids.

In the end, when the Binding is complete, they all look different, with special abilities they didn't have back on their home planet. Over time, we humans eventually just made them out to be these local myths, because why not, right?

Okay, it all sounds trippy. Again, I'm sorry. I stumbled into them in the woods that day, and I kind of . . . joined their party. There was a wendigo and a werewolf and a lady who can sever her lower body and fly. We had a centaur and a nine-tailed fox and Bigfoot himself, and I got to know this immortal guy they call the Harbinger. Went on quests with him and stuff. Helped them prepare for the end of the world because they knew the Hostiles were coming.

They didn't know when though, and this whole thing, this whole mess we're in right now, this all came as a surprise. And now the world is ending, and I'm still here, and you're . . . away.

I still have your Hello Kitty watch, though. I don't think I'll ever take it off.

I guess what I'm trying to say is that I messed up. I should've looped you in on all this—instead, I kept you away thinking I could protect you, then fed my saviour complex thinking I was some hero on a role-playing game meant to save the world.

I'm not.

At the end of the day, I'm still me, still the awkward Ava, still clinging to the hope that I'll actually make it out of the apocalypse alive and see you again, if only to give you your Hello Kitty watch back.

Until then, I'll keep this letter in my pocket, and when this is all over, maybe then I can give it to you. Maybe then, I'll tell you more about these myths I've been travelling with and their powers and my slip-ups and this guy I really like. Maybe then you can meet them too, and we'll laugh and hug and share stories and have sundaes again like nothing's changed.

Maybe then, you can make peace with the fact that I left you behind.

Maybe then you'll forgive me.

1

New Game Plus

There's a bunny on the ground.

I have no idea where it's been or where it's going, and does it even know that everything has gone to hell? Does it care that the world is ending, that the past six weeks have all been smothered wails and endless chasms, maelstroms in our nightmares and sandpaper on our tongues?

Does it care that death is our shadow now, chalking itself onto every wall in the dark?

Of all the things I've been training to find during the apocalypse—the right angle to slice through chinks in alien armour, enough warmth in a KFC when it's raining cats, dogs and monsters outside, and peace from the guilt of stealing the last Kit Kat from another survivor included—the most elusive has been the strength to cry for me.

I've been crying about a lot of things lately—this quiet mediocrity, the nothing of every calendar day. Searching for hope where there is none. Giving up. Making space for death with my head down low—welcome, stay a while, I've got nowhere else to go.

Sometimes, though, when something triggers a memory—the smell of singed corpses or the wheeze of the last breath or the thunder of a broken heart—I'm wrenched back to the sunshine of our high school days, of Cassie gushing about cheerleader practice and my co-op teammates trash-talking and Dad slamming the door on his way out.

The tears come then, and I don't even notice them until a rogue drop or two trickles onto my lips. I'd be doing something as mundane as tying the laces on my Chucks or doing a headcount of the refugees and the tears would come falling, and I wouldn't even know why.

It's happening again now, I think, out here in the open, in this empty playground in the middle of nowhere. School's out for the summer, but there are no kids, no squeals, no laughter. There's just me and this oppressive silence, pregnant with the weight of loss.

We used to think we were invincible, me and my friends and the games we used to play. The life we held in our hands, late papers and coffee, bike rides and messages, warm afternoons and regrets.

We staked our claim on each new day like we knew what we were doing, but the end of the world changes things.

And I feel lost every single day.

I scrub the tears off my cheeks with the back of my hand and finally decide to pick up the rabbit, but it leaps away back into the bushes like it was all a mirage. In its place, a small blade stabs into the ground at an ominous angle, the speed at which it was thrown narrowly missing the bunny by a fraction of an inch.

A shadow looms. He unceremoniously tugs the knife out of the ground, but he may as well have ripped the rabbit apart the way tragedy gnaws away at our frayed edges.

'One, you shouldn't be out here.' He's *not* happy. 'And two, you shouldn't have hesitated.'

And I look up at Connor, his glasses and his freckles and everything that used to be so sweet about him, now hardened and brutal and absolutely terrified, exactly like me.

Like I said. The end of the world changes things.
But most of all, it changes people too.

* * *

Connor doesn't say a word to me all the way back to camp. Five
minutes is all it takes to get to the playground, but a five-minute
stroll through an abandoned city is just the right amount of time
it takes to get killed.

I know he's mad at me. His jaw has been clenching and
unclenching like there's no tomorrow—which is honestly a big
possibility. Nobody knows anymore and there's no guarantee we'll
survive another day like this.

Which is why we're both on edge, on high alert, our eyes
darting back and forth as we sneak back into camp, every sound a
suspicion, every gust of wind a potential for death. I have nothing
but a blunt kitchen knife to defend myself in a world filled with
monsters, so paranoia is a good thing.

I can't help but heave a sigh of relief the moment we reach the
camp entrance and our two friendly-neighbourhood elf guards let
us in. Towering over us with their fists clenched and the haunting
horns on their heads, Eirik and Vidar look as menacing as guardians
in an apocalypse should. Their bare chests are puffed out like sheer
muscle alone can stop the monsters from coming, and their amber
eyes are trained on us as we slip past them into the camp.

Of course, 'camp' is just a fancy word for the makeshift
headquarters we've fashioned for ourselves, which is basically an
abandoned office building of what used to be a printer company
or something. Nobody needs toner during the apocalypse, so the
place is relatively untouched from all the looting and the rioting
and the killing.

Which makes it the perfect place to hide from all the evils
lurking in the darkness.

That's what Old Ester called them, the monsters. Back
when she was part of our barely surviving little party. Back when

we were camping out in a corner Huang Mart down the street. Back before the right chunk of her body got chewed off as she watched herself die.

There were more of us back then, but numbers tend to dwindle in an apocalypse. And while there's no flesh-eating virus that some big evil corporation has let loose in the city, or an army of the undead pounding at the door, wandering outside alone is equivalent to certain death. Which is exactly why Connor is fuming at me, staring at me now in my private quarters-slash-copy room on the second floor.

'What the hell, Ava.'

That's all he says. He whispers it, actually. With seething, loathing emotion. Because we've both survived life-and-death scenarios like this before, but all of our experience points and virtual levels mean nothing now. Our Health Points will not replenish, and our ammo and equipment will never be enough.

We stare at each other, locked in a losing battle of trying to be braver than the other.

It didn't use to be like this, like there's no space for a wayward smile, no room for whispered relief. Six weeks ago, I graduated from high school with my best friend Cassie—she was heading off to college with her boyfriend Roy and I was pining over Connor wishing he'd see me the way I saw him. There were video games and forest hikes, intimate cabins and meteor showers. It was the prime of our lives, until one seemingly harmless day changed everything.

We never did talk about it, Connor and I. It was as if recalling what happened to us made it more real, which only makes everything we lost even more painful. Besides, it wasn't like we could just sneak what happened six weeks ago into a regular conversation.

We ran over a zombie, which turned out to be a good guy, and then I was recruited by a group of mythological creatures in the woods to help them on a quiet quest to save the world.

I hopped from place to place with them for a while doing awesome side-quests naive little me thought was pretty cool, but then the Hostiles arrived on Earth, sent everything to hell and now here we are.

It's not exactly regular coffee-table chitchat.

Connor sighs and accepts defeat. He cups my cheek and strokes my skin with his rough, calloused thumb, as if trying his hardest to preserve what's clean and smooth and innocent of me, but nobody's pure—not anymore. We're all rough. We're all calloused.

We're all damaged beyond repair.

He pulls me towards him. I close my eyes and lay my head on his chest as he wraps his arms around me. I realize that my tears never really stopped falling since the rabbit appeared to me in the playground. The dried tears caked to my face match the grime and pain and sorrow on Connor's, and as we try to lock the agony away, he stifles a sob of his own.

Taking comfort in each other has always been what we've done best, and whenever we embrace, my heart just crumbles a little bit more each time. I look into those pained green eyes behind his glasses and see the little boy that took Cassie and me to school when we were kids, trapped inside this feigned bravado. I see him lost in there somewhere, struggling to get out, for the first time since everything fell apart.

I bury my face in his chest. 'I'm sorry.'

Connor looks around us, at the heartbreak and the destruction and the death.

'I'm sorry, too.'

2

Damage Per Second

The days aren't always this bleak. Moments of weakness are uncommon in our camp, mostly because everyone is so busy trying to be the warriors they are not. And when all you want to do is survive another day, the drama always comes last.

It's small and cosy, our camp-slash-office. Two floors, a pantry, three conference rooms and rows and rows of empty cubicles. I try my best to not look at the family pictures pinned to corkboards on most of them, knowing full well that those faces smiling at the camera are mostly already dead by now if they were lucky. If they weren't, then hell has caught up with them—it's caught up with all of us.

Seven civilians we've rescued from the streets, and three of the elves Connor had with him when they first flew in from Europe. Even now I feel they never should have come here—never should have accepted this personal mission.

But if there's one thing I've learnt during all these terrifying weeks, it's that there's no room for 'should-haves'. Those things will kill you—if the monsters outside don't get to you first.

'Ava?'

A knock on the door to the copy room jolts Connor and me back to our senses. We break apart from the embrace.

'Back from the scout,' the voice outside the door drawls. 'You being naughty again?'

Connor sighs and pulls the door open, revealing the slender, six-foot magnificence leaning by the frame.

'I brought her back, Siv. No need to make a fuss.' Connor brushes past the elf without looking at her and disappears down the stairs.

Siv raises her eyebrows at him. 'He's grumpier than usual. Piss him off, eh?'

'I was just . . . I needed to be alone for a while.'

'Juicy.' She twitches her pointy ears that are long enough for their tips to reach just above her head. 'If you wanted to die, Ava, you could have at least slept with him first. Everyone knows he's cranky because you just won't give it up.'

'Siv—'

'I mean it, luv,' she shakes her pixie-cut hair that's as vibrant green as spring foliage. 'The world is ending. Might as well let off some sexual steam, yeah? And I can think of no better candidate for you than brooding Eddie Redmayne over there.'

I'm about to tell her off when her last comment cuts me short. 'Eddie Redmayne?'

Her ears twitch again, the way they inevitably do when she's excited. 'Yes, dear. From the *Harry Potter* spin-off films. And that one about Stephen Hawking.'

'So, you're a movie buff now, are you?'

'I've always *adored* movies.' Her otherworldly yellow eyes sparkle at me. 'And yes, your precious little Connor looks exactly like Eddie Redmayne.'

I find it hard to believe how a warrior elf could have had free time and public access to all the movies Siv claims to *adore*, but my life has changed so much that I don't know what's possible and what's not anymore. Plus, I've only known Siv for a month and a half; what do I know about her life?

'I'd appreciate it if you stayed out of my sex life, thank you very much,' I roll my eyes. 'How was the scout?'

'Two blocks away. Top floors have all been destroyed, but the ground floor is intact. Used to be a café, I think. Looks untouched now. I'll need to make sure it's secure though, for the next rounds.' She pushes away from the door frame she's been leaning against and stretches her long arms up over her head. My eyes trail down her body.

I can't help it. Siv is as enticing as pop culture makes out all elves to be, with the tall, lithe frame, the lean muscles and the curves in all the right places. That's how they all are, I guess, and it doesn't help that Siv only has a makeshift wrap around her full breasts and a similarly haphazard wrap around her groin.

She says she just can't be restricted by clothing, because they're all hardwired that way, the elves. They live their lives in the woods totally free of baggage, and that includes pesky underwear. They're completely naked, all day, every day. The only reason Siv's put anything on is for the benefit of us humans roughing it out here with them.

'We can all move in by tomorrow morning.' She scratches her ab-tastic tummy, at the battle scar right across her belly button. There's no shortage of them, the battle scars, because Siv isn't like those pristine beauties from the *Lord of the Rings* movies—at least, the ones I've seen. I've played my fair share of elven characters in video games too—and they're usually all about the range.

But Siv—well, Siv's a tank, a war-worn warrior, and those horns above her head only make things worse. Hers sprout ominously from the back of her head and curl forward with the pointed tips near her jaw, only the left one is partially lopped off. Another casualty of war, I suppose.

'That's good news, Siv. I'll go tell the others.' I make a move to brush past her when she touches my shoulder and stops me.

'Ava. You should know we're running out of places to hide.' Her topaz eyes bore themselves into mine. 'I want to save all these refugees just as much as you do, but . . . we can't keep going on like this.'

My heart constricts, but I shake away the feeling and ignore her. 'I'll go tell the others. Where's Luna?'

She sighs. 'In the pantry.'

I walk away before she sees me tremble. Denial is a good thing sometimes.

Setting that last thought aside like a Quick Save state I'll get back to later, I march into the pantry as a pair of monstrous, bat-like wings heave into view. The leathery skin and the pointy bones punctuate this horror vibe Luna's got going on, but then she tucks those wings behind her as she turns around to face me, flashing a relieved smile—it's the only thing that keeps me warm these days.

So, the bat wings. Luna is a manananggal—a supposedly malevolent entity that takes to the skies abandoning the bottom half of her body on the ground, her guts and entrails hanging out of her torso as she preys on unwitting victims in their sleep. Filipino folklore tells you to smear salt on the severed bottom half of her body to make sure she perishes by the time the sun rises—but like most of our human beliefs, Luna is nothing like her reputation says she is.

But when have humans ever been experts at accepting the supernatural and the unknown?

'*San-san ka nanaman pumunta*,' Luna tuts at me and wraps me in a too-tight but too-welcome squeeze. 'Don't ever do that again.'

'I'm sorry,' I mumble against her sundress, as grimy as I am now with the way we've been flitting from place to place. Luna used to be so radiant with the carefree dresses she used to steal from random travellers. Now, there's no more feeding her odd little hobby—all we have are the clothes on our backs and our limbs intact, if we're lucky. 'Any news?'

She sighs and lets me go, flapping her bat wings behind her for a beat. '*Wala*. It is . . . difficult to find information. Ferals everywhere.'

'I know. Thank you for trying.' I brush my fingers against the silver bracelet on my wrist. 'We'll have another go tomorrow.'

Luna eyes me fiddling with the bracelet, then shoots me a look like she doesn't want to be the bearer of bad news. But, like I said, denial is a good thing. It's the only emotion keeping me going right now, and I'll need it to survive another day of uncertainty.

Because I *need* to save as many of these people as I can. Each and every one we encounter on the streets, every lost child, every grieving mother, every heartbroken friend.

And since I can't find him, it's the only thing left for me to do.

* * *

'The human tongue doesn't have the capacity to properly pronounce what our race is called.' Brad tucks a strand of his silver hair behind his ear and smiles at me. 'This skin, this body, it's nigh indestructible.'

'Like Superman?'

'Like Superman.' He bares his fangs, and suddenly we're right back inside Cassie's cabin in the woods, in the bedroom where we first met.

'Ava, Ava, Ava,' he shakes his head. 'There is no such thing as a vampire.'

And I'm standing there looking into his blood-red eyes, sinking deeper and deeper into them until I see that his eyes are actually sinking, sinking into their sockets, sinking into his skin.

'Brad?'

'We know they're coming, but we don't know exactly when, not even Ethan.' His eyes keep sinking until all that's left are two holes gaping back at me.

I cup his face with my hands. 'Brad!'

'They invade, and they take over. They kill every last inhabitant until they're the only ones left.'

Horror grips me as his beautiful, perfect face shrivels up. Then, three blades shoot out from his torso, his blood seeping out in circles, coating his whole body with a dark red mess.

'We will win this war, or I will die trying,' his voice fades.

I grab his shoulders, his arms, his hands, but everything I touch slips through my fingers like sand until there's nothing left but the ghost of Brad's smile on his face.

A pair of familiar black wings unfurl from behind him, and I realize that Luna is hovering just above his head, her bottom half missing. The clicking and the moaning and the grumbling resonate all around her—the unfortunate sound she makes whenever she takes flight—but this time, it's an elegy, a mourning hymn, a lament. She stretches her bat wings and envelops Brad in them, looking very much like an angel of death come to take my love away.

All the ghosts in the clearing of the forest where I first saw him—the Pure—they come for him now, and did they never get the chance to Bind, to find peace, to live among us as they always wanted? Brad said he would save the world, and I believed him. Am I wrong to still believe him even now, now that he's gone, now that there's nothing left?

They scream. That horrible, shrieking, screeching, eldritch scream, their language, they sing it together in a morbid melody, a dirge for the death of my heart, and it's only when they all disappear before me that I realize I'm screaming too.

I wake up.

Dread. Someone really is screaming, in the middle of the night in the silence of our camp, which can only mean one thing.

They're here.

They've found us.

And it's only a matter of time before we're all dead.

I seize the kitchen knife from under my makeshift pillow and bolt out of the copy room, making a mad dash down the stairs. The screaming is coming from the back door leading to the fire exit. I try to ignore all the questions that my frightened nerves are asking—how could we have possibly been compromised despite our sealing this place shut as best as we could?

The power lines have been down since last week, and the little electricity left fluctuates—some nights they're on, some nights, not. Tonight is one of those deathly dim nights, but our eyes have become so used to the gloom that we hardly ever wish the lights were on.

Besides, the dark shields our eyes from all the horrors of the world, at the very least.

Unfortunately, this time, not enough darkness can dim the horror that I see before me when I reach the fire exit.

Mr Ngan has always been a timid man. We found him four days ago by the alleyway near the bakery, trying to sneak his two little girls inside to loot for bread that has long been looted. Siv rescued them just in time before a pack of adolescent gangsters stormed the place and performed one of their rituals—real, demonic cult stuff. Sacrificing maidens and all that.

Now, Mr Ngan looks as rabid as the monsters we've been running away from all these weeks. With Connor pinning his arms behind him to restrain him, Mr Ngan is thrashing around, his eyes bulging out of their sockets, his screams as otherworldly as the monsters outside our door.

So it was *his* cry of anguish that woke me from my nightmare. Although, honestly, this waking world is just as much of a nightmare. These days, I hear a lot of the kind of screaming that Mr Ngan is doing right now.

Because through the wide-open, fire-exit door, out in the lot where this printer building's office parking used to be, are Mr Ngan's twin daughters, sprawled on the floor like forgotten ragdolls, beautiful, still and lifeless. Both the girls lay soaked in pools of their own blood and guts, their faces frozen forever in expressions of fear, shock and resignation, the lower halves of their bodies chewed right off.

They are still holding hands.

If I'd had a proper meal at all these past few days, I would've already thrown up. It's the first time I'm thankful I haven't had anything to eat today save for half a cracker.

Mr Ngan has gone mad with grief.

'Let me go! Damn you!' he roars. 'My babies, my babies . . .'

My heart breaks. Over Mr Ngan's uproar, I hear Siv grunting outside the door, and only then do I realize that whatever chewed off the twins is still out there, just a few paces from where Connor and I are standing.

My heart completely grinds to a stop when I hear the shrill, high-pitched growls.

Ferals. Two of them. Siv won't stand a chance.

Connor's split-second shock gives Mr Ngan the opportunity he's been waiting for. 'I'll kill them! I'LL KILL THEM ALL!' A savage now, he breaks free of Connor's grip and charges through the open door, past Siv and straight at the two Ferals towering over him.

'NO!'

Siv reaches out to try and grab Mr Ngan, but in his grief-stricken state, he's deranged. Siv hesitates, weighs her options and makes a decision. She dashes back into the office towards us, slams the door shut and bolts it.

The topaz of her eyes is almost luminous in the dark.

Then, she hisses. 'Go.'

Connor and I sprint up the stairs. We know what all this means. Ferals don't hunt in pairs—they hunt in packs. We have mere minutes before the rest of them close in and chew us up as they did the twins.

'What's happening?' Mr and Mrs Cai, the elderly couple from last week's rescue, peek around the door of their conference-room quarters, their eyes wide.

Connor ushers them back in and squeezes their shoulders. 'We're moving out. Now.'

They don't need to be told twice. They shuffle back into the room and gather their essentials, while I race towards the other conference room. I open the door to find Mrs Gonzales and her daughter huddled together in the corner.

Little Didi peers up at me with her big brown eyes. 'Are we . . . are we going to die?'

I swallow. 'No, sweetie, not while I'm around.' I feign a sunny smile that I hope is as cheerful as whatever shred of happiness I have left in me. Then I turn to Mrs Gonzales, 'But we need to move out. It's time.'

She nods and coaxes Didi to get a move on, grabbing their overnight bag that's already prepped and ready to go. I have a similar pack in my copy room, which is the only thing I grab on my way out. None of us ever fully settle in whenever we find a new camp, because surviving means never staying in any one place for too long.

By the time we all head back down the stairs, Siv has already taken her stance by the entrance to the office building. The two elf guards, Eirik and Vidar, bring up our rear, their faces grim. Luna is out on her nighttime food raids—the only time she can sneak past humans more easily—and won't be back until daybreak. Without her, we don't have enough raw firepower to take on two Ferals.

I try to ignore the fact that Mr Ngan's screams from beyond the back door have stopped, and wish in my heart of hearts that I can somehow give his family a proper burial. I can only hope they're all together now, wherever they may be.

The three elves exchange glances, sharing an unspoken agreement.

And, unprepared and unarmed and exposed for the kill, we head out the door.

3

Timed Challenge

Two months ago, the vibrant alleyways of this now-unnamed city wouldn't have looked like this. The all-pervading darkness has choked the life out of the streets, and the city, gasping for air, is forced to make way for debris and death.

The weight of the sky presses down on us. The air leaves an unpleasant taste as we rush through without a sound. Like upturned earth after the rain. Like swallowed coins and metal. Like fresh, fresh blood.

Two blocks away. That was what Siv had said, about the next camp she had scoped out for us. Luna should be able to find us there when she returns from her raid. Back when the world was what it used to be, on a normal day, it would have been a breeze to walk two blocks with our helpless group of civilians.

Now, we're zigzagging past the cars abandoned on the road, ducking down whenever Siv signals to us to hide and popping into the byways whenever we have the chance. The whole city is deserted—or at least, it wants to seem that way. Even as we're moving along, I can feel furtive eyes boring into the back of my neck, watching us and probably wondering why we're all out here just waiting to get ourselves killed. Once or twice, I almost catch a pair of disembodied eyes from behind shuttered blinds, but they disappear as soon as I see them.

But we've got other pressing matters at hand.

My thundering heart is all I can hear. I keep telling myself over and over that we're almost there, almost at the café's ruins, almost to safety. I tell myself I can't die here, not while everyone and everything is a mess. And it almost works, calming my nerves, as I watch Connor up ahead of me, assisting the Cais behind Siv. Mrs Gonzales is in front of me and is as unravelled as I am, but I can see she's doing her damnedest to be strong for her little Didi. I'm almost convinced we're going to make it to the next camp safe and sound.

But then it happens.

As if in slow motion, the Kirby plush in Didi's hand slips, its little accessory bell tinkling as it rolls down the alleyway to my left.

And Didi darts after it.

Mrs Gonzales screams.

My flawed rationality kicks in. The grimy pink toy is nearest to me now, and I sprint towards it just as Didi picks it up and holds it tight against her chest with her little arms. Then, she stays there, unmoving, staring up at the darkness of the alley before her. I'm just about to hoist her off her feet and carry her back to our line when I see exactly what it is that's keeping her rooted to the spot.

It raises itself up on its hind legs and lets its long arms dangle just above the ground as a gorilla would. Towering over us now, out of the shadows and in the moonlight, I see it—actually see it—for the very first time. Its whole body encased in a hard exoskeleton, segmented from its underbelly and heavily armoured like a reptile, it looks like a cross between a velociraptor and a bull. The horns curl out from its temples towards its forehead, and as it lowers its maw down to our level to devour us, I'm amazed at just how much detail my brain can take in on the brink of death.

I guess that's how my brain panics. It shuts out everything and focuses on the mundane.

The Feral opens its mouth, baring six-inch fangs, revealing a second inner mouth that looks eerily human. As its long, slimy tongue unfurls from within, all those Resident Evil games I've stayed up way too late to play flash before my eyes.

And then it happens. My adrenaline. It's the single, most volatile weapon an untrained survivor like me has. The moment the Feral's tongue is within reach, I whip out my kitchen knife and slash.

The tip of the tongue flops down in a slimy mess at our feet.

The Feral roars.

Just as I'm about to chuck my useless kitchen knife at it in a final feeble bid at survival, two arrows slice through the air and pierce the Feral's eyes with razor-sharp precision. It growls even louder—now, unable to see anything, it swings its long arm right at us, aimless and desperate.

I grab Didi. My whole body is still high on adrenaline as I run back. Eirik and Vidar rush past us, directly at the rampaging Feral, reloading their bows and risking everything. I push away the thought that my recklessness might just have cost them their lives, but I hold Didi tighter against my body now, carrying her back to our terrified group.

Silence. Despite the horrible mistake we've just made and everything falling apart, we're all silent, panicking and hurrying but not daring to make a sound. I run side by side with Mrs Gonzales, whose wide eyes send me a look of gratitude, but there will be time enough for that later—if we ever get to safety.

There's nothing but our hushed breaths and frenzied footsteps now as the Feral's screams grow fainter and fainter behind us. I resist the urge to look back, to check on Eirik and Vidar, and instead whisper a desperate plea to the powers-that-be that they make it out of the battle alive.

Siv skids to a stop in front of us. She yanks open the doors to the seemingly untouched café she told us about, and Connor ushers the Cais in. Mrs Gonzales and I follow suit, and as I brush past Siv through the door, her amber eyes follow me with flickers of both determination and fear.

She's not sure if we'll be entirely safe here, but it'll have to do.

The moment we're all inside, I lay a quivering little Didi back in her mother's arms. Connor and I glance at each other, and we get to work.

We've been through this before. Each new place has to be made secure—has to be bolted down and sealed shut. The two of us spread out, securing windows, twitching the curtains and blinds into place and locking every door. Although the Ferals might be death incarnate, they have poor hearing and even poorer eyesight.

So if you're not directly in their line of sight, or you make as little noise as is humanly possible, you might—you just might—keep the monsters at bay.

When it feels like we've covered all our bases, Connor and I make our way back to the centre of the dining area where our little family has assembled, holding one another, trembling and crying and mourning our fates in silence.

And Siv stands tall by the door, clenching her fists and trying to look like an invincible force that can protect us all, keep us safe and fight off all the demons that could crash through our temporary sanctuary at any moment.

But, with her brothers out there and us in here, I know she can't.

She can't do it alone.

I think about how Eirik and Vidar will try to lure the Feral as far away from us as possible, with no idea when and if they'll ever make their way back to us and I realize that it's just as Siv said.

We can't keep going on like this.

* * *

Cassie once told me that the Brady Barbecue Grill empire's influence is a global entity, with at least one Brady product in every household.

'It's almost as if we have eyes everywhere, if, you know, grills had eyes.' She had flipped her golden curls over her shoulder and giggled. As the only daughter of a grill tycoon, Cassie was pretty much set for life—Mr and Mrs Brady always made sure she had everything she needed and wanted, including a group of personal bodyguards we jokingly called The Brady Bunch.

She was right in a way. I mean, right now, I would have loved for their products to have eyes, or ears, or anything at all that would help me talk to Cassie again, or make me feel some semblance of closeness to her, or help me remember what it felt like to have my best friend by my side every single day.

Eyeing the dusty Brady Barbecue Grill now in the kitchen of this abandoned little café, I want nothing more than to have Cassie with me. Of course, having her here only means she'll be in just as much danger as I am, instead of tucked away in a Brady safe house somewhere, probably in some super-remote mountain, or super-secure bomb shelter, far away from all this chaos.

Mr and Mrs Brady *had* to whisk her away when the attacks began. They just had to rescue the princess of their empire. And I'm only a little bit disappointed that Cassie didn't even put up a fight, didn't even protest, didn't even put up a token resistance to stay here with me.

But Cassie didn't have any fight left in her. Not since the attacks. Especially not since Roy.

Everyone deals with grief differently.

'You have to eat *some* time.'

I jump the moment Connor walks into the kitchen, my nerves still jittery from our narrow escape about five hours ago. None of us ever had the guts to fall asleep no matter how tired we were.

For me personally, it's partly because I'm hoping the elf brothers will burst in through the front door any minute now, triumphant and unscathed.

I'm still not giving up hope.

'Thanks, Connor, but I'm not all that hungry.'

He takes one look at my trembling hands on the old grill and hands me half a protein bar from his pocket. 'Sure, you aren't.'

I don't need much convincing. The lure of the sugar proves too much to resist.

Connor looks at the grill that I've been staring at and grins, 'Thinking of getting one for yourself?'

With a heavy heart, I try to smile back through the sugary goodness in my mouth. Of course, when Mr and Mrs Brady rescued their princess on their private helicopter and carried her off to who-knows-where, they left behind their prince right here with me.

'You should've gone with them.'

The lopsided grin fades. 'Ava, not this again—'

'I mean it,' I swallow the last of the protein bar. For a second, I consider mentioning Annie, this colleague he was living with in London, this unknown girl I was insanely jealous of, like it matters at all now. I don't even know what happened to her, and Connor never really said anything about it. Instead, I go for something closer to the heart, 'Your parents need you, Connor. *Cassie* needs you.'

The mention of his little sister's name makes him hesitate for a split second, before he says, 'I need you more.'

I have been pining over Connor ever since that epic *Nebula Battles* tournament, when I lost and he won and I suddenly had the urge to kiss him. That was when I realized how much I had fallen in love with my best friend's brother, how spending all this time with him and going on all those online quests had totally ruined my heart.

We hesitated. We skirted around our feelings for each other. Then he left for Europe and broke my heart. And then . . .

And then I moved on too.

But then there are all these . . . stirrings. We never talked about 'us' since the attacks, because how can anyone have the time or energy to deal with the heart when your life is at stake every minute?

That's where we're wrong, I guess. Because the more I realize that we could die in the next second, the more I feel that we should probably come clean and tell each other how we feel, *really* feel, before it's all too late.

Connor's still looking at me, those green eyes piercing and intense. I open my mouth but, as expected, nothing comes out.

Coward, I chide myself.

He pushes his glasses up his nose to mask his disappointment—or was it hurt?—and turns away. 'Mrs Gonzales says she can't thank you enough for what you did for Didi. And for letting the little one have your half of the meal tonight.'

And with that, he walks away.

Meet me in Ming Yu Outpost.

That was the only thing Brad had wanted to tell me, apparently. *Meet me in Ming Yu Outpost.* Dazed, bleeding and with his right leg chopped off, Brad simply wanted me to meet him in Ming Yu Outpost, if we ever got through all this.

When we got separated during first contact, Luna had found him bleeding to death, unable to Bind, unable to find a new Host, left for dead by a Hostile in the middle of nowhere. He was too injured to do anything other than breathe, Luna had told me, and all she could do was tend to him for a few days while he breathed and breathed and breathed, all consciousness lost. The Hostiles' magnetic blades weren't meant for human bodies, I was told—because of our frailty we would've ended up torn apart and ripped limb from limb, or, if we were lucky, those blades would have made us explode upon impact.

Brad survived because he's the Harbinger, but even so, how could the Hostiles be this efficient?

It was only on the fourth day that Luna could finally leave his side for a bit to call for help, and help did come. Luna got in touch with Brad's elite guard, who had an army general from Ming Yu Outpost in tow—along with disturbing news for good measure. Sightings of the Lightbringer—their noble leader who had brought them all to the safe harbour of Earth when their planet was colonized—had cropped up, and Brad was going to do everything he could to find him.

'I am to take care of you until my last breath,' Luna held a hand over her heart when she found me, recovering from an injury of my own in Connor's camp. 'The wendigos will take Brad to one of their brothers in Shanghai. *Manggagaway.* Shaman. Their master who taught them their healing art. He will recover there.'

I sat up from my makeshift bed and winced at the pain in my side. 'I'm going to see him.'

'*Hija,*' Luna shook her glorious locks at me. 'When he is well enough to stand, he will visit the Outposts, the Strongholds. In different parts of the world. He is to ensure all battle stations are ready. The Harbinger must prepare. In the meantime, I am to make sure you somehow learn how to fight—he says it was your request.'

It was. I wanted him to teach me to fight but, given his condition, the task to teach me had to be delegated to someone else.

'He's not going to do it alone.'

'He is not. He will end his trip in Ming Yu Outpost, to find truth about the Lightbringer sightings. "Meet me in Ming Yu Outpost," he says to you. We ride when you are well.'

Twenty-eight days later, stowed away on a barge to China, we docked to find the port a bloody mess: Ferals and humans and myths in the middle of it all. Nothing was as we expected, and the road to Ming Yu Outpost has since been long, winding and hopeless.

Meet me in Ming Yu Outpost, he had said. It's been six weeks since I last saw him. I don't even know whether he's alive or dead.

When the days are long and the nights are hard, I think about my healer wendigo friend, Harley, and his dude-ness, how he's doing and if he's ever going to get rid of his tacky 'Surfin' USA' T-shirt. I think about Jimmy the Bigfoot and his fluffy coat, how his gentle nature is going to help him survive this terrible world, and if he will ever be able to keep his heart from being corrupted by the despair all around us. I think about Ethan and his foresight and his books, and will he ever find the peace he's sought so desperately ever since the humans shunned him centuries ago? I think about Kiyoshi and her solitude that's forever beyond reach now, and of Big Bad Wolf who's . . . no longer here.

I spent so much of my time travelling with these myths that it feels like they've been ripped away from me, and now I'm left this hollow shell that's as empty as it was when all of this began.

And what about Aunt Steph? Did she make it out of the fiery pits of hell, some way, somehow, safe from the horned beasts and armoured Hostiles, the monstrous Handlers and their seething, livid eyes? Did she ever find a safe haven for the survivors, away from all the carnage, worrying about her adoptive daughter and wondering why she never heard from her again? Did she manage to somehow scavenge enough food for herself, or did she have to fight for survival against the desperate lashing out of her fellow man? Or—

Or—

Denial is a good thing.

I sigh and gaze down at the grill, running my thumb across the small Brady logo and wishing things were back to normal, to Cassie and I having sundaes at Marcello's and Roy helping his dad out behind the counter.

Everyone deals with grief differently.

And I don't think I'm doing a very good job.

* * *

At some point, I must've fallen asleep against the grill on the cold, kitchen floor, because I wake up with aching muscles and the grill's pattern etched on my cheek. The morning sun laces through the gaps in the already boarded windows and burns small spots on the floor, but it's too late for sunshine now, too late for anything but the dark from here on out.

I emerge from the kitchen and see everyone is fast asleep in the various nooks and corners of the dining area. Connor's head is resting on the cashier's countertop; even asleep like this, there's not a shred of peace on his face. Siv is still standing guard by the door, and by the way she's looking out through the peephole with laser focus, I know that Eirik and Vidar still haven't come home.

A pang of guilt grips my heart with such intensity that I breathe out a small whimper, and Siv turns to me.

'They'll be here, luv. It's not your fault.'

Sometimes, I wonder if those topaz eyes can see right into my brain. She grins to put me at ease and then looks at my cheek. 'Looks like you were pretty intimate with that kitchen grill last night.'

I smile in spite of myself. 'How's the water supply?'

'Only in the bathroom,' a gentle voice wafts in from my right. Luna is back from her raid and desperate to keep her exhaustion tucked out of sight. 'Weak, but good enough.'

Relief washes over me. 'Thank you. I'll go ration our food supply.'

'No.'

'Excuse me?'

Luna sighs like she doesn't know what to do with me. 'Siv?'

The elf strides towards me on her long legs and places both her hands on my shoulders. 'Everyone else is still asleep. Let them have their rest. You can ration the food later.' She nods, and I'm mesmerized by those powerful horns on her head. 'Right now, we need to talk about our options.'

'Um. Okay?'

'Ava,' she grips my shoulders tighter, 'I'm telling you this warrior-to-warrior. I know how much you feel like it's your responsibility to save all these people, but you can't save everyone, not in this war.'

I burn up. 'I don't—'

She shakes her horns. 'I get it. I do. The Harbinger isn't here, and you're feeling useless, and you think the only way to help his cause is to do the impossible and save every single soul you meet out there. But the truth is that he has left us with very specific orders for when the Hostiles arrive.'

Siv narrows her amber eyes at me. 'The contingency, Ava, is to carry on with the plan with or without Brad. We all have our orders. We knew this when we came with Connor, and we'll make sure it gets done.'

'What do you mean?'

She sighs. 'Brad knew that things would get chaotic the moment the Hostiles arrived. But he also knew that we have the home-court advantage and that long-drawn-out wars usually end when the losing side's supplies get depleted. In short, whoever has the supplies that will last for the long haul, wins. I believe he got this strategic idea from you. At least, that's what the Avem—the Stymphalian birds—tell us.'

From what I remember of our Greek mythology class, the Stymphalian birds have bronze beaks and metallic feathers, which they use to rip into humans when devouring them. Of course, Siv isn't referring to the birds from the labours of Heracles, though— Luna once told me that these birds are their people's messengers, and if they can relay the random strategies I used to spew out like I knew what I was doing, they just might be the closest thing we have to the Internet right now.

Siv releases my shoulders and scratches behind her long ear. 'I hope you understand, Ava, that the plan was for our pockets of resistance to build camps, gather supplies, and *stay put wherever we are*. We are to act as the supply lines that will replenish our warriors wherever they are in the world. Which is why we just . . . we can't keep moving. As soon as my brothers return, we need to stay put and start setting up camp.'

Siv gives me a moment to take this all in, before she continues, 'I know that part of the reason you want us to keep moving isn't just to save as many people as you can. I know that, deep down, you're hoping to run into him, somehow, by some miracle of fate. This may be difficult for you, but you have to understand that we . . . we're not even sure if he's still out there. We're not even sure if he's still al—'

'He's alive.'

I look at her, right into her alien eyes. She sighs again.

'Do you know how Connor found you, Ava? That day in the woods?'

That day. In the woods. When the Hostiles arrived, and Brad was—

Brad was . . . lost.

'You were a dreadful mess, all bloodied up from the explosion. Connor tended to you until you fell into an exhausted sleep, while we charged through the forest into battle. Only after the initial wave was repelled, we took you back to camp that night. I wanted to send you away, to one of the wendigos, to receive proper healing. But Connor refused to let you go anywhere, demanding

instead that the healers be brought to you. He said that he hadn't
travelled all that way and gone through all that trouble just to get
separated from you again.'

I bite my lip.

'Connor told me plenty of things. When he didn't hear from
you again after your last phone call got cut off, he investigated the
mysterious occurrences himself. He eventually found his way to
us, to our hidden cove, and sought our help. He has . . . a good
soul. A remarkable human. We wanted to rally to the Harbinger
too, so we mounted an expedition to find you. And find you we
did—and so much more.'

Siv glances at the front door again, then back at me. 'And
then, when the world fell apart, he chose to stay with you.'

Connor. In another time and another place, things might have
been different. 'And you, Siv? Why did you and your brothers stay
behind too?'

Siv smiles. 'I'm a sucker for romance movies, you know.
Connor is a good man, and I am loyal to him. I'd like to see his
story through, yeah?'

I look down. I never asked them to come with me, although
I'm glad they did. It used to be just me and Luna who were in
danger, but now I'm jeopardizing others too—the Cais and
Mrs Gonzales and poor little Didi.

Siv places her hand on my shoulder again, this time less urgent
and more sympathetic. 'I'm sorry, luv.'

I glance around at our temporary family huddled together,
asleep and at peace. There's no space for silly insecurities here,
for hidden agendas and pointless searches and this version of me
where I can still be a kid. There's no room for the old me whose
only concern was finding herself in a sea of high school faces,
the girl who only had her video games with her whenever the
weekend waved its magic, the Ava who kept fidgeting with her

hair because she liked her best friend's older brother too much to stay still.

When the invasion blinked into existence, I had to leave all childish things behind—but there's no manual for any of this, no in-game tutorial to prep me before the main campaign, no training phase for me to get a hang of the controls pre-match.

And I realize that with the way I've been dealing with the loss all around me, I can't save everyone when I can't even save myself.

4

Escort Quest

Four bread rolls . . . a cracker . . . two more protein bars . . .

I sigh. This isn't going to work. Rationing our food supply always leaves me feeling desperate right after, because nothing is ever enough. The way things are now, we'll probably last through tonight—and if I stretch it out, until tomorrow morning. And that's it.

The carton of canned goods was in Mr Ngan's backpack, which he was wearing when he . . . went away.

We are so screwed.

'The twins probably opened the back door by themselves and slipped out when Mr Ngan was asleep.' I'm surprised when Mrs Gonzales comes over to me, because she has never spoken to me before. None of us really do. As a group, we're all travel buddies, yes, but we never talk—*really* talk—to each other. I guess there's this unspoken agreement to not get too attached to one another because, eventually, someone always gets chewed up or maimed or cut in half. And our numbers will dwindle until nobody's left or someone gets replaced, and there's no point in trying to get to know someone you know will only be with you temporarily.

It's the sad, morbid truth.

'Why you humans are divided among yourselves is absolutely baffling,' Brad had told me once. 'This world you have is such a magnificent place. If my people were still alive, I would have relished and cherished everything.'

I ran my fingers through his unkempt silver hair. 'Earth is such a big place. You can't expect every single person here to just magically get along with everybody else, what with all the different cultures and worldviews and stuff.'

His face twisted. 'Our people are different too, but that's all we have—each other. For humans . . . I will never understand it. Perhaps an invasion is just what humans need, to force them to unite.'

'Maybe. But you're going to save the world, remember?'

He grinned with childlike ingenuity, those sharp fangs glistening. 'Yes. With you as my top priority.'

'Mmm. My hero.'

'Do you want to know what I think?' Mrs Gonzales snaps me out of my soul-crushing reverie. I guess bonding with me is Mrs Gonzales's way of thanking me for rescuing Didi. I nod, and she continues, 'I think Mr Ngan's twins saw a *duende*.'

I hold back a sigh. Figures. Luna had once told me that popular Filipino mythology tells of small, malevolent spirits that lure children out to dangerous places under the pretence of wanting to play with them, only to lead them to their untimely deaths. This is what people believe about the duendes, but, according to Luna, duendes are nothing more than the Pure that Bind with local children hosts.

So, yes, they're real; but, no, they aren't malevolent. And neither is Luna, who flies around with the bottom half of her body missing. In fact, Luna is one of the sweetest beings I've ever had the pleasure of knowing.

But I can't explain all this to Mrs Gonzales. I don't think she can handle the truth—that what we've always believed to be mythological creatures are actually ghost-like aliens who Bind with dead human hosts to survive on Earth.

It's complicated. So duende it is, then.

'They lurk in the bedroom walls of little children, and strike when they have the chance,' Mrs Gonzales continues, her tired, bloodshot eyes widening in macabre enthusiasm. 'A duende must have drawn them out into the parking lot. That is why they opened the back door.'

I guess it's a variation of the Latin American lore. 'Of course. That must be it.'

'Of course, it is,' she shakes her head. 'Poor, poor, sweet little things. And Mr Ngan, oh.'

I look down at the table in front of me and go back to rationing our food, when she speaks again, 'Did you used to live in China too?'

'My Aunt Steph did. Connor and I came from America.'

Mrs Gonzales heaves a sigh, as if mourning for us. 'You should've stayed there instead of moving. There's nothing but death here.'

I think about our hometown, when I came to from Connor's camp and received the horrible news. How even our little town in the middle of nowhere hadn't been spared this nightmare. How going back to Canyon Falls only meant finding everything destroyed, Cassie rescued by her parents, and Roy . . . gone.

There was nothing but death there too.

I hand her a roll of bread plus my half for Didi. She refuses and smiles, 'Thank you, *hija*. But you should eat. Didi and I will be okay.'

'But Didi looks so frail and clearly shaken from last night,' I insist. 'Your daughter needs this more than I do.'

She smiles again and to my surprise, gives me a quick hug. I think of Aunt Steph missing and tear up. 'You're such a sweetheart . . . but Didi is not my daughter.'

So that explains why they look nothing alike. 'She's . . . not?'

She shakes her head. 'A few days after the initial impact, I found her alone on the street and took her in with me. But I do have a little one just about her age, though. Or *had* rather. Her father was bringing her home from school when . . . when the attacks happened.' Mrs Gonzales swallows a lump in her throat. 'They never made it home. Not that it would have been any safer in our apartment. When those things crashed through, I barely had time to run for my life . . .'

I hold my breath. I had been with Brad and his elite guard when the Hostiles came, and in Connor's care when it all went down. I can't even imagine the shock of the people who were trapped indoors, or out on the road, just going about their daily lives and coming face to face with the Ferals out of the blue, wholly unprepared and suddenly fighting for their lives.

I clasp Mrs Gonzales's open palm. 'They could still be out there, you know. They could still be alive.'

She shakes her head again, smiling through her tears. 'I may not know much about what's happening to us right now, but I know in my heart when to accept things and to let go. And right now, I'm happy knowing that my family is at peace at last and away from all this.' She takes a deep breath. 'I have Didi now, and because of you, she's still alive. Thank you.'

Mrs Gonzales takes the allotted portion of bread for her and Didi, smiles at me and leaves.

And I think of Aunt Steph, whom neither the Brady Bunch nor the Stymphalian birds could find, and I somehow try to believe she's safe somehow, somewhere. That she must've been at work when the Hostiles arrived; that the Russian government would've done everything in their power to save their top mechanical engineers because they're irreplaceable and invaluable and needed to be protected at all costs now that the unthinkable had happened.

I know she's safe the same way I know that Brad is safe and alive out there somewhere, despite the three fatal stab wounds on his body and his right leg missing.

Sometimes I wonder whether I can even tell the difference between stubbornness and blind hope.

I pick out more bread rolls to give Mr and Mrs Cai, when the door to the café suddenly bursts open. My mind and my heart both scramble to fit shock, fear, hope and more fear into each other, because the door is wide open and we're vulnerable and unprepared and we're all going to die.

But standing there in the doorway are the two elf brothers, alive and well.

My heart explodes.

We rush to them just as Siv slams the door shut. Eirik steps forward. I've never seen his face look so determined yet so afraid at the same time. With his long horns shooting straight up into the air, he looks almost as menacing as the monsters outside.

I'm about to ask what's wrong when he turns to me, narrowing those amber eyes.

'We found something.'

* * *

A warehouse.

Stable, intact, naturally fortified. It stands isolated, past what used to be a train station, half a day from here on foot. But that's not even the difficult part.

Although perfect for setting up the supply camp that Brad had apparently tasked his men to do, the warehouse is surrounded.

By Ferals.

And the elves want to claim it.

From across the cramped dining table, I gape at Eirik and Vidar and conclude that these two must have run mad for sure.

'Plenty of space, a storage shelter in the back and away from the main roads,' Eirik continues, slouching to keep his horns from scraping the ceiling. 'The Harbinger would have chosen the exact same place.'

'Temporary stronghold,' grunts Vidar, nodding. His horns, on the other hand, curl around the top of his head like a wreath. 'We protect family. Siv sneaks in. Ava slithers through the vent. If caught, Luna kills Ferals.'

'If caught? *If caught?*' Connor slams a fist on the table. 'If you think I'm letting you send Ava out there like she's some kind of expendable ocular equipment, you're—'

'There's a vent access to the warehouse. It's the only way in without alerting the Ferals, and we'd rather not face them head-on if we want to survive. Ava's the only one small enough to fit through it.' Eirik waves a scarred hand around. 'It's purely a reconnaissance mission, Connor. Ava slips in and out. Tells us what we're up against inside. And then we formulate a plan.'

'No. Absolutely not.'

'I'll do it.'

Connor glares at me. 'Excuse me?'

'I'll do it.' I look around at the three elves boring their amber eyes at me, and at Luna, looking confident as heck that she can take on the Ferals out the door. Then, I return Connor's glare with as much intensity. 'Siv will be with me, right? I'll be fine.'

Siv grins. 'I did train you well, didn't I, luv?'

'Don't encourage this,' Connor snaps at Siv. 'Ava—'

'Great. That's settled, then.' I straighten up as Connor releases an exasperated sigh. 'Just let me know when we're leaving. I'll be in the kitchen.' I walk out without giving anyone a chance to say anything else.

The moment the kitchen door swings shut behind me, I lean against the Brady grill again and take a deep breath. This whole thing is so much bigger than me and my personal mission. I'm no hero and I sure as hell am no Chosen One—Kiyoshi made that perfectly clear while she was all up in my head the last time. But I do what I can, and I *choose* to be here. And right now, the best I can do is survive and help others survive with me. I can't save the world no matter how many times I've done that in my meaningless virtual quests, but I *can* do my part in my own way, in my own circumstances and with whatever resources and skills I have at the moment.

Right now, that special skill is to be this sneaky little girl who's small enough to fit through a vent. I'll do what I can.

Besides, there's only so much you can do in an apocalypse. You try to eat, try to sleep, try to escape and then wait it out until the next time you need to escape again. Waiting it out can take forever, so training every single day for six weeks is the most productive use of your time.

That's what I've been doing, every night, whenever Siv has the chance. All my gamer skills are useless now and I'm not physically strong enough to be the fighter I want to be. But I *can* be crafty. At Luna's request, Siv has taught me to master the art of slipping through unnoticed, of weaving in and out of trouble, of honing my Agility points so that I won't have to confront monsters head-on.

If there's one thing my years of gaming have taught me, it's how to maximize one's build and exploit the enemies' weaknesses. If I'm not powerful enough to defeat the Ferals on my own, the least I can do is be agile enough to evade them.

If that means sneaking in through an access vent, then I'm totally up for it.

Connor bursts through the kitchen door a minute later, and we engage in another pointless glaring match. It's always been like this now, and why can't we be honest with each other? In the midst of all this anarchy and chaos, why can't we just say what we want to say?

He heaves another long, drawn-out sigh, then perches on the counter across from me. 'When Cassie and I were younger, we had this nanny. She was nice, but she had the most fantastic stories, which she'd sneak into our conversations every now and then. Cassie didn't care for them, but I found them fascinating.'

I fold my arms across my chest. The Brady Bunch shared a few folk tales of their own, when they picked up me and Cassie sometimes. I'm not surprised.

'One day, she told us about this malevolent spirit, this . . . invisible creature with a penchant for knocking on people's doors, hoping they would answer. This thing would lurk about and learn a certain family's habits, their names, their lifestyles, their personalities and their quirks. When she was little, she says she heard her mother's voice downstairs, calling her down for dinner. But when she checked, there was nobody there— her mother wouldn't be home for three more hours.' Connor glances at the door. 'On another night, she was watching TV in the living room, and there was a very definitive knocking at their front door and the voice of her brother, telling her to let him in. But her brother was right there across the room in the kitchen, and he heard the whole thing. She swore it was all true.'

I tilt my head. 'What happens to the people who answer their doors?'

Connor tugs at his high ponytail. 'She said the night takes them. Like it's a living, breathing, seething entity, luring unwitting souls away, never to be seen again.'

'That's . . . interesting.'

'One of the Brady Bunch had a similar story,' Connor continues. 'He says his father was cursed one day with a sudden and excruciating pain in his side after demolishing this old building at a construction site. None of the doctors could identify his "sickness", and he was soon plagued by nightmares of wayward children who were lost and couldn't find their way home. According to these children in his head, he had destroyed their home and was now responsible for them, burdened forever with the onus of their care. Haunted and sick, he eventually went insane.'

I hoist myself up on to the counter beside Connor. 'Aunt Steph had one of those stories too.' I try to shake away the sadness of still not knowing where she is. 'She told me that a friend of a friend of a friend encountered a *Ba Jiao Gui*. Legend tells of these "female, banana-tree ghosts" holding a baby and wailing beneath a tree at night. For some strange reason, they're very good at predicting lottery numbers, and this friend tried to invoke one of them. He tied one end of a red string around the accursed banana tree and the other end to his bed, binding the enchanted woman to him. True enough, he won the lottery—a whopping ten million dollars—but before he even got a chance to enjoy the spoils, he went missing that very night. The next morning, his neighbours found a trail of innards from his house leading towards the fated banana tree. A fresh, teardrop-shaped, blood-red banana heart was blooming, and right under it, his severed head.'

'Creepy,' Connor shakes his head. 'It's always "a friend of a friend", isn't it?'

'Aunt Steph had a close encounter herself, actually,' I wave an open palm into the air. 'When she was a little girl, she liked watching birds fly by, and there were quite a lot of birds in her province. One day, when she wandered into the forest during an afternoon of intense hide-and-seek, she chanced upon one of the most beautiful birds she had ever seen. Perched on a low branch, the bird had its back to her; it had rainbow-hued plumage with a long tail that reached down to the ground. She was struck speechless by the magnificence of the bird until it turned towards her. One by one, all nine of its necks turned, at the end of each neck, a leering, wide-eyed human face, grinning manically at her.' I smile. 'She swears by the story of the *Jiu Feng* to this very day.'

We both fall silent. I can tell that Connor detected the break in my voice at the mention of Aunt Steph. But sitting side by side with him like this and recalling urban legends, I almost forget about the end of the world.

'It's incredible, all that's happened to us in the past weeks,' Connor whispers. 'I mean, these myths . . . who would've thought they'd be real?'

It's not entirely accurate. Sure, these myths and creatures might be real, but they're not even remotely close to what humankind assumed they were. They're the kindest, noblest, most peaceful, alien refugees, Binded with human hosts to survive in this world after they had been driven out from their home planet by the same Hostiles who are now taking over Earth.

Even after all the time I've spent with them, getting to know them, making friends with them and falling in love with one of them, I still can't wrap my head around it.

'All those video games taught us squat, huh?' Connor breathes out a soft chuckle, and I offer a weak laugh along with him. All those late nights owning co-op missions. Levelling up. Hunting for treasure. Going on quests for the ultimate weapon or the rarest equipment or the most indestructible armour. Battling zombies and aliens, demons and ghosts, armies and gods.

Nothing compares to the monsters outside. Saving the virtual world countless times has done nothing to prepare us for saving the actual world now.

'I'm not backing out, Connor.'

'I know.'

'It's the only way I can move on.'

'I know that too.' Connor glances at the broken Hello Kitty watch on my wrist—*Cassie's* Hello Kitty watch. My eyes dart towards the tiled floor in shame. Connor mercifully doesn't say anything else.

He heaves himself off the counter to the floor. With one final feigned smile at me, he heads out the door.

I perch there on counter, still staring at the floor, and just when the silence begins to choke me, Siv calls me from the other room.

Time to go.

5

Player Two

'. . . and Kirby can run and jump, and shoot fire and ice and bombs, and he can fly, and he can swallow bad guys and the big boss too.'

Didi shakes her plush toy at me, and I'm amazed at Kirby's ability to continue to smile despite all his grime and dirt.

'He can swallow everything. He can swallow the monsters outside. He can save us all,' Didi bores her innocent eyes into mine.

'Of course, he can, sweetie,' I squat down and grin at her. 'Which is why you need to keep Kirby with you at all times. He's here to protect you, to protect everyone. He's the only one who can keep us all safe. So, don't lose him, okay?'

Didi squeezes her chubby, little fingers tighter around Kirby's round body and beams at me, nodding. I open my arms wide and she eagerly jumps into my embrace.

I swore a long time ago to not get too close to any of the survivors we met out here, but Didi . . .

Didi is special.

I reluctantly let her go, knowing that if I held her against me a second longer, I would burst into tears. She hops onto the back of the bus in which Mrs Gonzales is seated on the floor. She nods her gratitude at me.

I straighten up. Our small family is hiding out in an overturned double-decker bus, out here in the stillness of the parking lot of the warehouse, which is just a few paces in front of us. Parked cars have long been cannibalized for working parts, and grocery carts are strewn about, their contents spilt across the lot among the garbage and blood. Whether the blood is human or not is unknown, but judging by which side is currently winning in this war, I can venture a pretty accurate guess.

I make my way down the aisle and pass Eirik and Vidar, who are staying behind to keep everyone quiet and hidden until we say it's safe to follow. Luna squeezes me in another literally breathtaking hug, flashing me a light-hearted smile, like there's nothing to worry about.

Connor stands by the door to the bus, his jaw set, gritting his teeth and smouldering at me. Whatever was left of that quiet, geeky, green-eyed boy that all the college girls were going ga-ga over is gone now, leaving only the runaway heir of a corporate empire and this mask he's desperately trying to hide behind.

But I guess I understand. I didn't use to be like this, either, but now I'm just as lost, looking forward to the day I can be myself again.

I lay a hand on his chest and feel his muscles ease up slightly. 'I'll be fine,' I say, and throw him one last smile before I hop off the bus.

Siv is waiting for me right outside. Her amber eyes are luminous in the shadow of the night, and tonight, like many other nights, I surrender my fate to her very capable hands.

'Ready, luv?' She smirks for my benefit, like we're just about to go off on a fun and exciting adventure instead of plunging into enemy territory where we could very well end up getting chewed to bits.

I nod. 'Let's go.'

The crisp breeze hits my face with a ruthless intensity as we race through the lot, ducking down behind piles of scrap metal every now and then. Sneak in. Sneak out. Quiet as a church mouse. Slip in. Evade. Stealthy in sight and sound. Don't get seen. Don't get caught. Don't die.

Siv has taught me everything, but as we draw closer to the warehouse, the horrors of the night reveal themselves to us.

We crouch behind a small cargo crate. 'What are they doing?'

Siv narrows her eyes beside me. 'Waiting.'

The pack of Ferals prowls around the warehouse, antsy and on high alert. It's rare for Ferals to congregate and stay in one place like this; they're usually out preying on humans and destroying cities. Right now though, it's almost as if they've chosen to stay here instead of following their natural predatory instincts. Almost like they're keeping something out, or keeping something in. I'm not sure what's making them so anxious, but whatever it is, the answer's got to be inside.

'There.' Siv points to the easternmost corner of the structure, at the access vent Eirik and Vidar were talking about. It's an easy break-in—I've infiltrated far more fortified buildings in the past few weeks, stealing and looting as surreptitiously as I can, to feed our family of survivors whenever we get the chance. But none of those structures had a pack of edgy Ferals patrolling the area like this.

We creep even closer to the entrance until the very ground shakes with a Feral's footsteps. I can almost feel the heat of the angry breathing directly overhead; but, as I've been trained to do, I clamp down on my rising fear and keep it shut tight. This is neither the time nor the place to go into panic mode.

'This is as far as I can go,' Siv whispers. 'Remember—stay low, stay quiet. If they can't hear you, they won't look for you. And if they don't look for you, they *won't* see you. You've got this, luv.'

I nod like I know exactly what I'm doing. Then, with a deep breath, I'm off.

The raptor-like features and the armoured exoskeleton only emphasize how resilient the Ferals can be—after all, they managed to survive crash-landing on Earth in those meteorites. But despite being hardy enough to withstand that kind of an impact, Ferals have something in common with our earthly bovines—and it's not just the horns. Their poor vision comes with even poorer depth perception, so even if I'm right in front of them, crouching as low as I can get on the ground, the eight-foot monstrosities can't tell if I'm a shadow or a pothole without lowering their creepy heads to check. But if I don't make a sound, they won't have any reason to double-check anything—which is the ultimate goal, because I definitely don't want to see those fangs parting to reveal that humanoid set of teeth in their inner mouths. Once is enough, thank you very much.

I eventually reach the access vent without a fuss, and I take a quick moment to glance back at Siv. She pops up her tousled head of green hair from behind a crate momentarily to flash me a quick thumbs up.

The vent is covered with just a flimsy screen, and I thank my lucky stars that it's not one of those screwed-in metal grates, which all the Arkham games always have Batman break into. He makes quick work of those bars with a swift kick, then they bust open for him to sneak up on bad guys and kick their butts. But I'm no Dark Knight. If I were to kick a vent like a badass, I would probably fracture my foot.

The screen makes a small squeak as I pry it open, but thankfully, I'm in before I figure out whether the sound alerted the Ferals or not. The dust and the dark greet me inside, but what did I expect? It's a vent. It's not exactly meant to be an alternative entrance.

The irony isn't lost on me as I crawl my way through the claustrophobia-inducing shaft. Almost every third-person action-adventure game is bound to have the main character crawl through a vent of some sort as a necessary rite of passage in his/her quest to save the world and stuff. Who would've thought I'd be doing the same thing?

If only it were that glamorous.

After the seemingly unending tunnel and my paranoia that the vent would end up leading nowhere, I see the exit up ahead. I shove the screen a few times with all my might until it bends and comes apart, and I crawl up and out from the ground.

Coughing out the dust and rubbing the filth from my eyes, I scan the scene in front of me. It's a warehouse, all right—but it's anything but empty. Furniture, equipment and all kinds of supplies are stacked up high almost to the ceiling, seemingly untouched and un-looted. The vastness continues down the hall, everything neat and orderly, everything in its place. There are signs up above leading to the various areas of the establishment, showrooms and items for every part of the house.

It's a warehouse-slash-showroom, and it's all still here.

Why hasn't this place been ransacked just like every other structure in the city? Why is it completely empty with no one else around? And more importantly, what the hell do the Ferals want with a fully stocked furniture shop?

I shake my head and try to get my bearings. I had noticed a door by the access vent a while ago, a fire exit that opened only from the inside. If I could just locate it and maybe let Siv in . . .

Bingo.

I shuffle towards the fire-exit door and fumble at the latch. The moment the rusty metal makes a small squeak, something else clicks at the back of my head.

Dread.

The air thickens. A grunt through gritted teeth, a few curt words in Mandarin. Cold, hard metal presses against my messy bob, and I freeze.

'You open that door, you kill us all,' a gruff voice growls against my ear, translating his earlier words for my benefit. Like it would change anything. Like it would matter. Like the final meal before the executioner flips the switch.

The gun cocks. 'Now. Do you mind telling me what the hell you think you're doing?'

* * *

Living room. Dining room. Bedroom. Bathroom. I squint to adjust my vision to the dark, as we pass by every section of your average-sized house inside the gargantuan maze. Even though the power is out, everything is in its place—except that once in a while, I spot in my peripheral vision a hidden family or two, crouching low. Refugees, survivors, innocent civilians—they've barricaded themselves inside this furniture store, and it's almost as if there aren't any rabid aliens just outside waiting to devour us the instant we make a mistake.

The air, though—the air betrays all false pretence. Dripping with the stench of desperation, the silence reminds us all with a cruel finality that death is just a slip-up away.

In my case right now though, that slip-up is closer than ever, with a gun pointed to the back of my skull as I'm led down the huge hallways. We stop in the hall of checkout counters—it's been transformed into a makeshift base of operations of some sort, and there's activity here.

All the checkout counters have been pushed back against the walls to make room for the men and women in the middle of the area, huddled in groups of threes and fours, heads bent down as they pore over random documents. Everyone's deep in discussion about . . . something, and I catch a few words in Mandarin here and there thanks to Aunt Steph. But even with all the urgency, a hectic kind of silence reigns over the room, a controlled, low buzzing that doesn't dare get any louder.

I catch furtive glances and stolen whispers, until I'm led to one of the counters against the wall. There's a bigger group of men surrounding the table, and a handful of them either have pistols holstered at their hips or knives strapped to their sides. For a second, I wonder if there's an armoury around here somewhere, a rich depository of murder weapons laid out right next to the fancy silverware.

'Leslie,' barks the guy with his gun to my head.

The sea of men around the table parts just wide enough for me to catch a glimpse of whatever it is they're all fussing about in there—equipment, parts, some sort of tech?—and then someone emerges from within all the commotion. A skinny, middle-aged woman with narrow eyes and a square jaw walks over to me—or, rather, wheels her way towards me. Her long locks are neatly tucked into a long, single braid that reaches down to her hips. There are stumps where her knees should be and as she angles her wheelchair towards me, her lips tug sideways, pulled taut across her hard face.

They start speaking in Mandarin, and I fire up the back recesses of my memory to catch the context clues like my life depended on it—and in this case, it actually did.

Aunt Steph, don't fail me now.

'What's this?' Leslie snaps.

'Says she's a refugee, with a group of survivors hiding in a bus down in the lot. Couple of seniors and a little girl,' my hospitable host snarls. 'Says she's looking for a safe place to stay, but I caught her trying to pry open the fire exit.'

The woman frowns at me. 'How'd she get in?'

'Through the vent.'

'Yes, but *how*? Those abominations have the place surrounded.'

'I—well—'

'My friends,' I interrupt the discussion in English, and they try to hide their surprise that I understood their conversation. 'They're pretty handy. They helped me sneak in because they *know*

things. They know more about all this—all of *them*—than any
of us do.'

The woman—Leslie, was it?—waves her hand. My captor
lowers his gun and walks away. She raises an eyebrow at me, then
switches to English. I almost sigh in relief. Almost. 'What kind
of friends?'

'Just friends. Special friends. They have abilities . . . they're not
like us. They're not from around here.'

'So they're exactly like the monsters trying to kill us.'

'They're *not*.' I clench my fists. 'It's . . . complicated, but they're
here to help. We just want a place to stay, for the civilians who're
with us. My friends are stronger, faster. They can help you with
whatever it is you're trying to do in here. They're resilient, and
they can fight.'

'Can they fight those things outside?'

'Well, they'd rather not, but—'

'Then they're of no use to me,' Leslie swivels around. 'If
you're looking for sanctuary, you're welcome to stay here. My men
will protect you. But I can't let you go out and fetch these *friends* of
yours and compromise everyone else's safety. Humans who want
in, stay in. And if your *friends* are half as capable as you say they
are, then I think they'll do just fine out there without our help.'

'No, you don't understand—'

'Leslie,' a blonde woman from the huddle rushes up to her,
trembling, 'there's . . . activity. We think it's emanating some sort
of signal . . .'

'*What?*' Leslie growls at the woman and speeds back into the
circle, and when everyone parts to let her through, I see it.

Laid out on the table, propped up nicely and proudly on display
for all these men and women trying to study and understand it, is
a piece of a Hostile's armour.

But it's not just any armour—it's a chunk of a Hostile Handler's
arm plate, one that the elf brothers and I personally witnessed in

action when that pack of Ferals tore down our temporary fortress and Old Ester got chewed in half.

'Get rid of it!'

Every head in the makeshift command centre turns to me, incredulous, as Leslie swivels back around to face me. She grits her teeth. 'I beg your pardon?'

'The arm plate.' My heart batters against my rib cage and a cold sweat breaks out all over my body. Siv told me exactly what these were when we first encountered one, and it's not something I ever want to see again. 'It's not safe, keeping that thing in here. That's exactly what's luring those Ferals outside—it's made to *control* them. They're confused and waiting for their Handler's command. You have to destroy it!'

'I'll do no such thing!' Leslie is livid. 'And you, *girl*, you'll do well to know your place. You're an *outsider* and you *dare* presume to tell me what to do when I barely know anything about you? What do you—'

Everyone screams. Leslie is cut short as I grab the pistol hanging by the hip of the guy nearest to me, and without a moment's hesitation, I level the gun point-blank at Leslie.

And shoot.

But I'm not aiming at her.

The men around us scamper away in shock as I fire bullet after bullet at the Handler's beacon on the table. I don't have enough firepower to completely destroy the thing—the armour is more resilient than that—but I can at least disable it long enough for us to get rid of the Ferals outside. And maybe, just maybe, that small window of opportunity will be enough to keep everyone alive.

Just as the beacon flickers and goes dead, someone snatches the gun from my fingers and yanks my hands behind me.

Leslie hisses. '*You little*—'

A low rumbling followed by a crash outside instantly springs everyone into action. I watch in awe as more armed men spill out into the hall and the unarmed ones immediately retreat to the back area where I came from. No orders are made, and Leslie issues no commands, but everyone knows the drill, everyone knows their place. They speed through protocol as the back entrance is barricaded to protect the civilians I passed by a few minutes ago, and every man and woman with a weapon turns to the huge double doors right in front of us, poised and ready to defend.

Leslie throws me a look of pure loathing one last time before she wheels into position herself, probably blaming me for whatever this is, disturbing the peace and rattling their so-called sanctuary.

Another crash and a series of high-pitched growls, this time just beyond the walls, bring me to my knees as the ground trembles. Debris rains down inside the warehouse. A quick succession of heavy thuds reverberates through the floor, and I can't tell if the pounding I hear is coming from outside or from within my own heart.

I think of Luna and Siv and Didi and the Cais and Connor and shitshitshit we're all going to die when the double doors burst open, flooding the light-starved hall with blinding moonlight. I barely even have time to register everything that's happening when Connor leaps in and skids to a stop right in front of me.

'Ava, we have to leave. *Now.*' Connor grabs my shoulders as a few of the men who have recovered from the blast cock their guns at him. 'Something attacked the Ferals—they've gone crazy and the elves are—'

The loudest, most ear-piercing shriek tears through the building. I zero in on the looming shadow hurtling towards us with inhuman speed from behind Connor. My body reacts on pure instinct as I shove him aside at the very last second and we crash down to the ground just as a Feral slams into the open doorway and slides down the aisle from outside. Everyone screams.

It's dead.

I wince. Connor helps me up, slowly, carefully. There's a stillness outside now—a sudden and all too eerie stillness. My eyes are transfixed on the Feral's corpse in the middle of the warehouse's checkout area, its eyes rolled shut, its jaws agape, its humanoid inner mouth split wide open and the long, reptilian tongue lolling out to one side. The stench strikes my nostrils as its warm blood oozes out from all sides of its exoskeleton.

The tremors stop. Rocks crumble. Slow, tentative steps from outside approach the gaping hole in the wall where the doorway used to be. As the dust settles, a lone figure appears in the opening, silhouetted against the night.

Stray strands of pristine silver hair dance in the wind.

My heart stops.

The dark, blood-red eyes lock into mine. In an instant he's in front of me, sucking out all the air from my lungs and filling it with life-giving hope and euphoria at the same time.

The kiss. It's the first thing he does.

'Ava—'

Brad doesn't finish. Because, standing tall beside me with his fist shaking, Connor punches him right across his perfect face.

'Who the *fuck* are you?'

6

PvP

Everyone remembers the exact moment they came.

Each person here, every widow, every orphan, every survivor, remembers exactly how it happened, what they were doing and where they were when the Hostiles arrived. It was instantaneous and terrifying, and there wasn't enough time in the world to prepare for it, to prepare for anything. In bed, on the road, at work, in school—none of it mattered. Everyone suffered, then grieved. They're still grieving, and you can see it and hear it and feel it, in the muted pockets of conversation, in the hushed tones and the averted eyes—afraid, afraid, afraid.

The suicides. They grow more horrendous by the day. The crimes against fellow man, more grotesque.

Everything is futile. The generals and the priests and the scientists, all these advancements in technology—everything pales in comparison to the magnitude of the apocalypse, the invasion and the looming finality of our deaths.

Will we return to the stars, they ask? Will we laugh, will we cry? Will we see it, feel it?

Will it hurt?

Walking past all these refugees now, these families without a home, forced to live out the end of days with strangers in this loud and unforgiving world, I can't help but wonder: can Brad do anything at all?

Brad.

All this time, from believing he's alive to accepting that he's dead to going crazy about it—I just can't deal with any of this right now.

But then there's that incredible kiss . . .

I swallow the lump in my throat and ignore the heat searing through my body. The world is ending. There are more important things than my raging hormones right now, and that includes repairing the damage to the checkout area's wall.

According to Siv, they were all patiently waiting for me when Brad soared down on his flying mount and just started kicking ass. At the sight of their Harbinger, Luna and the elves sprang into action and showed the Ferals who was boss with renewed vigour. Then, all hell broke loose, and while Connor couldn't understand anything, he sped off to bring me to safety, and the rest—well—

The rest is history.

The Handler's arm plate beacon has been deactivated. Brad is in one of the order-processing terminals right now with Leslie and a few of her men, discussing war stuff (and explaining everything) along with Luna and Siv. Eirik and Vidar are helping with the repairs on the wall because, while no other Ferals should come prowling about now that their Handler's beacon is gone, it's only a matter of time before other non-friendly human folks barge in to loot our little gold mine.

I have no doubt that Brad's natural charm will take care of diplomatic matters from here on, because he's just that dignified— so much so that the whole punching thing with Connor didn't even merit an equally violent response from him.

Connor. In this time of momentary peace, he's my top priority right now, and I need to sort my heart out if I don't want to lose him forever.

Just as I knew I would, I find him in one of the micro-showrooms in the living-room area, a computer workstation with a Mandarin sign painted against the wall. With what little I know of my mother's native tongue, I think it says something along the lines of 'The Ultimate Gaming Space'.

He's in the black, swivel chair, staring at the non-functional desktop monitor in front of him.

'I'd kill to have this kind of a set-up in my apartment.'

He jumps at the sound of my voice. I flop down on the beanbag chair beside him and he swivels in my direction.

'Just imagine how many campaigns we could win with state-of-the-art equipment and absolutely no fear.'

He chuckles. 'I'd never leave this chair.'

I wrinkle my nose at him. 'Not even to shower?'

'Not even,' he taps the imaginary headset around his ears. 'You wouldn't know about it, anyway.'

We share a small laugh, and I stretch out my legs in front of me. Showers are a luxury we can't afford while on the run. I glance down at myself, the sweaty black top and the torn jeans and the grimy Chucks, and I suddenly feel exhausted.

Connor's green eyes are trained on me, as he unconsciously sways a little from side to side on the swivel chair. He scratches at a spot on his neck, and my eyes travel to his Adam's apple, more prominent now than it was before all this. His jaw is squarer, his resolve firmer. His brows are more furrowed, his shoulders more defined. Gone are the classy turtlenecks and elegant tailored blazers he used to sport as the only son of a Fortune 500 company mogul. But even now, in his plain shirt and jeans and still with his long hair gathered into a high ponytail, he's still Connor—my best friend's older brother, my ever-reliable gaming partner, my friend.

We've skirted around our feelings before, but there's no skirting around it now.

'So . . .' I clear my throat. 'That's Brad.'

Connor winces. 'That's Brad.' He shakes the pain off his fist. 'I got that.'

I flash him an embarrassed smile and he shoots one right back. Then, he leans back further into the swivel chair and sighs. 'Do you remember that day when we had that last video call?'

Of course, I do. I was with Brad then, trudging through the woods with my feelings all up in the air. I missed Connor so much and so badly, and when my phone's battery died and our call ended, I felt like my heart ended too. 'Yeah.'

'I spoke to Cassie before that. She told me all about the retreat and that you got all weird after she mentioned Annie's name.' Connor looks down at his palms. 'That was a confirmation of sorts, I think. At least for me. That these . . . feelings I had been having for the past year had turned into something else. That even though I refused to let myself believe anything, you were, apparently, feeling them too. And it drove me crazy.'

He clenches his fists. 'I remember thinking, "how do I deal with this? What am I supposed to do now? What am I supposed to say?" I went from fear to anger to more fear and confusion. You were this beautiful, amazing girl who spent all this time with me and didn't even realize just how wonderful she was, and I was so stupid to throw all that away.'

I had been pining over Connor for most of my senior year, so I know exactly how this felt. There was nothing but pain there.

'Your presence roared at me, Ava. You wrenched my attention away from everything and everyone else, every single day.' He leans forward and rests his elbows on his knees, his head drooping. 'You always said you were in the shadow of Cassie's light, tagging along for the ride. But you were all I could see, Ava. You always were. And it frustrated me that none of these high school boys even knew how to be around you. Whenever I went to your events or saw you with Cassie's cheerleader posse, I felt the sheer injustice of it all, of why it couldn't be me, why it couldn't be us.'

'Connor . . .'

'I should've fought for you. Instead, I let my insecurities and heaps and heaps of stupidity get in the way, so I came back too late. I was so damn afraid of losing your friendship that I lost you, all of you, altogether,' Connor's voice breaks. 'I guess I've grown so used to running away . . . from my family and from my feelings, that I screwed it all up when it mattered the most.'

Beyond the invasion, what happened—what *really* happened—in these past six weeks? When I graduated and Connor left, it almost felt like it all went downhill from there, and all of a sudden it was a 'before' and an 'after', and me, forever in between. Connor was everything that slipped away from me back then—he was everything I couldn't have, a missed phone call, a missed bus stop, a missed embrace.

I take a deep breath to steady myself. 'I liked you, Connor; I really, really did,' I lower my voice to a whisper now. 'It was overwhelming, physically and emotionally, carrying all these feelings for you without knowing what to do. You were the first boy I ever liked, but I couldn't sit around waiting and wondering if you'd ever like me back. So, I moved on.'

I close my eyes. 'At first, it was hell, but after a while, when I thought I couldn't take it anymore, it happened. It got easier. I found that I didn't think of you as much, didn't yearn for you like my heart was going to split in half. But the thing was that I didn't know I was over you until I met Brad.'

Connor sighs then, long, drawn-out, tired. 'Right,' he chuckles. 'Brad.'

I raise my eyes to meet his then, and Connor is still Connor but everything has changed.

'Maybe it was all timing, but it is what it is,' I shake my head. 'You'll always be the guy who constantly beats me at *Nebula Battles* without even breaking a sweat. We'll always have that, but I'm sorry, Connor. I really, really am.'

'Don't be. Don't ever say that.' The wetness pools dangerously at the corners of his emerald eyes, but he blinks it away and shrugs. 'Whatever this is, whatever happened or didn't happen between us, you're my friend, and nothing will ever change that. Those summer afternoons, those games. We'll always have them.'

How wonderful it must be to occupy a space in someone's thoughts, someone's memories, to be so spectacularly special that you're worthy enough to compete for the limited real estate in someone's heart. To share a moment in time with someone from your childhood, empty phone cans connected by strings, perfectly shaped hands to fill the space between your fingers.

'Do you want to know what I felt when I found out where you were?' Connor whispers, and I shake my head. 'Regret. For all the things I should have said and done before all this.'

I look down at my hands. There had never been time for a lot of things, and now there isn't any time at all.

'But do you know the first thing that popped into my mind when I found you? That you're alive—and that was all that mattered,' he continues. 'That's all that matters to me now—that you're alive, that you're here. And that your heart is beating, Ava, even if it beats for someone else.'

* * *

'So, it truly is a stronghold after all; only the Ferals weren't trying to keep something *in* so much as something was *drawing* them in,' Eirik says to me as he hands two boxes of miscellaneous household goods over to Vidar, who grunts.

'Handler beacon. Foolish humans.'

'Turns out Leslie and her men have been keeping these civilians safe here for the longest time, with no way out or in,' Eirik tilts his head to one side, his horns almost snagging against a low-hanging sign. 'They've been studying the beacon since they arrived, without knowing that it was sealing their fate the longer they had it with them.'

'Well, it wasn't *all* bad, was it? I mean, those Ferals skulking about outside certainly did their job—it kept rioters from looting the place. I mean, look at all this stuff,' I gesture to the shelves around me, as Eirik grabs more boxes of supplies to hand over to Vidar standing outside the storage room. 'It's an apocalypse-survivor's dream in here.'

'And if we play our cards right, it'll stay that way,' Siv marches back into the storage room just as Eirik slides out to give her some room. With me already inside and Siv like the proverbial bull in a china shop in this cramped space, we couldn't possibly fit another battle elf here. 'We'll need to fortify it, protect it from both Ferals *and* human cults. We'll welcome any refugees who wander in, but all in all, this'll make a fine camp. The Harbinger is pleased.'

'Leslie and her men are cooperating surprisingly well,' Eirik grins at me. 'Whatever it was you told her when you were in here must've made an impact on her.'

Vidar swings a huge sack over his shoulder and grunts again. I swear I could almost see wisps of smoke spiral out from his nostrils. 'Ava. Good.'

The elf brothers nod at me and leave, and I turn back to Siv, who's nodding her horned head.

'Things didn't turn out exactly as planned, but everyone's safe—the Cais, Mrs Gonzales, Didi. You did good, Ava. It's all good.'

I sigh. 'I just wish I could have done more, honestly. There wasn't enough time to explain everything when you guys suddenly started kicking some serious Feral ass outside.'

'There'll be time to do more later,' Siv glances at the doorway over my shoulder, grinning. 'Besides, I think you have to attend to something more important right now, luv.' She wiggles her eyebrows and squeezes past me.

I turn around to follow her, frowning, and freeze.

'Harbinger,' Siv bows her head at Brad by the door. He acknowledges her greeting with a nod and she leaves, but not before winking at me behind Brad's back.

Brad steps towards me with a pronounced limp he didn't have before, then he shuts the door behind him with a soft thud.

And just like that, we're alone again, after what feels like eons apart.

The red eyes stare at me with hunger and it's stuffy and cramped and all too hot in here. My stomach churns, leaps, and then something else replaces the feeling entirely—something wild and just as ravenous.

Every step he takes to close the gap between us feels like slow and exquisite torture. He lifts a finger, two, and strokes my cheek, light as a feather. He traces my lips, my jawline, my collarbone. The space between us trembles and my breathing turns more laboured as his eyes flicker down to my lips for the briefest of seconds.

He leans his face down towards mine. I part my lips to meet his, but instead he hovers near my neck, his hot, shallow breaths tickling my skin. He brushes his lips against my neck and smiles, teasing, frustrating. I know he's mocking me about the whole biting my neck thing, back when I thought he was this vampire who'd suck my blood at the first chance he got, before he told me that vampires didn't exist, before . . . any of this.

But here he is now, the first time we've seen each other since that horrible day in the forest, and he's restraining himself. Just to mess with me. But for all my self-control, I can't resist him. Not when he's like this.

When he feels he has tortured me enough, he makes contact. My eyes roll shut. He looks up from bruising my neck and stares at me, his blood-red eyes swirling pools of desire.

'Hi,' he hisses.

'Hi,' I gasp.

His lips claim mine in a dizzying flurry of passion, and I kiss him harder until his back slams against the door of the storage room with a thud. His lips twist into a wry smile at my aggression, and a pleasured growl rumbles from his throat when we part.

We stay that way, our bodies entwined against the door, staring at each other as the world morphs back into place. My tears get the better of me, so he swipes a thumb across my cheek.

'You can hit me if you like,' he whispers, smiling. 'It wouldn't be a true reunion without you unleashing your wrath on me, would it?'

'I thought you were—'

'I know,' the crimson eyes soften. 'I'm sorry, Ava.' He wraps his arms around my body and I sob into his chest. He breathes in against my hair. 'I'm sorry.'

Everything overwhelms me then, because this is it and I'm just a kid and this is no game and there's nothing I can do. I remember the last time we saw each other, and all those times we spent before all this, how he smiled and told me it would all be okay and how I believed him.

Now we're all just stumbling over what's left of humanity, as the whole world strains to heave one last breath.

I mumble my frustrations against his chest. 'Fuck, Brad.'

'Language,' he tells me, just like he used to. And I smile, and then chuckle, and just like that, I can make it through another day.

'I saw you get stabbed. I don't think I'll ever get that image out of my mind.'

'Again, I apologize.' He sweeps a stray strand of my black bob away from my face. 'The Hostiles are . . . efficient.'

Cripple the enemy. Catch him by surprise. Divide and conquer. Classic gaming strategy. The Hostiles are efficient, and Brad's very noticeable limp is proof that he hasn't fully regenerated that particular limb just yet.

'To be quite honest, I barely scraped through—blood and blades and all. I suppose they hadn't expected me to survive the attack, so they didn't think to look for me when I took refuge away from the battleground. I was out for who knows how long.'

Brad takes my hand in his. He guides my fingers inside his shirt, and I gasp. Because there they are: three deep scars ploughed right into the middle of his torso; a glaring reminder that even Brad, the Harbinger, one of the strongest of his kind, isn't invincible.

'It would've been a slow and painful death had Luna not found me,' he continues. 'Those blades . . . they didn't have them before.'

I stroke the furrows against his skin and notice the almost imperceptible wince that sweeps across his perfect features. They still hurt, and I can't even begin to imagine how much pain he had endured while he was away out there, bleeding and alone.

'I'm just glad you're alive,' I shake my head. 'You're alive, and you're here. That's enough for me.'

'I told you to meet me in Ming Yu Outpost.'

'I got sidetracked.'

He peers down at my face, uncertain now. 'Ava . . . I'm not staying,' he says. 'I'm . . . looking for something. I'll make sure the humans here are safe with Leslie, but I hope you'll come with me.'

I cup his cheek. 'I'm coming with you.'

'Thank you.' He bends down and kisses me again, this time softer, gentler. He sighs into me. When we part, I see it—that cheeky, playful smirk that infuriated me so much back then.

'You know, you'd think I'd be this noble, self-sacrificing hero who makes a grand speech about your staying behind for your own safety. But I've been away from you before, and it was a rather unpleasant experience. I dare not go through that again. World's ending—perhaps I should give being selfish a try, shouldn't I?'

He grins. 'Besides, if I leave you behind, you might get swept away by a well-meaning, childhood friend or some such.'

I giggle in spite of it all. 'He's taller than you, you know.'

'Oh, I'm quite aware of his stature,' he winks at me. 'That punch was a good one, if I say so myself.'

7

Weapons Upgrade

'They held you at gunpoint, *hindi ba*? These lowly men?' Luna frowns as she twirls me around, inspecting every inch of me like I'm a piece of meat. 'But the gods smile on us tonight. I thought I would never see the Harbinger. But if they touch you again—'

'Luna—'

'*Di bale*,' she continues, 'you're still the most beautiful maiden on the battlefield. No apocalypse can change that, *no*?' She pulls me into a warm hug then, squeezing me tight against her voluptuous bosom. Her wings whip out with awe and power behind her back in a sudden explosion of wind and toppled-over furniture.

The men around us can't scurry away fast enough. If they're terrified of her *now*, I can't imagine how they'll react when she takes to the skies, leaving behind the lower half of her magnificent body, clicking and moaning, her guts and entrails hanging from her waist. She tends to do that a lot.

'There's news,' she folds her bat wings behind her, once again the epitome of elegance and grace, but with the power to rip you in half if she so desired. 'General Wu says we need to call the Longma to arms.'

'The Longma?'

'Magnificent creatures. You will see. The general has one as his mount when he came here with the Harbinger. Once more, it is fate, do you see?' she places a hand over her chest. 'We leave tomorrow.'

This was apparently the same general who told Brad and Luna about the Lightbringer sightings when we were in America, and had been kind enough to accompany Brad throughout his journey.

'There is also a . . . change of plans. The Handler beacon . . . it can be studied.'

'Are you serious? That was exactly what Leslie and the others were doing before we arrived. Who'd be naive enough to even bring it up?'

'Connor.'

'Oh.'

'After we rouse the Longma, we will bring them here for extra protection for the humans. But Connor . . . he is leaving.'

I frown. 'What are you talking about?'

'He is to fly to Qing Feng Outpost to work on the beacon. What do you call it?' Luna scrunches up her nose. 'Ah . . . reverse engineering? *Kasama si* Siv and some of Leslie's brightest minds. He will not be alone.'

The idea of Connor going on a trip with a hot elf tugs at my heart for a bit, but I brush it off. 'How will I know he's safe at the Qing Feng Outpost?'

'General Wu will be with him.'

I open my mouth to ask Luna to expound further when someone wheels into the fake kitchen Luna and I are in.

'Ava,' Leslie barks, 'a word?'

Luna cups my cheek and walks away, but not before giving her powerful wings another quick flutter behind her back. All the colour drains from Leslie's face as she watches her leave.

I can't blame her. It takes some getting used to.

'So.' Whatever it is she came here to talk to me about, I'm not exactly thrilled that she interrupted my discussion with Luna. 'What is it?'

'Walk with me. There's . . . a small gathering by the living-room showcase. A celebration, if you will.'

I study her face for a while, her jaw firm and her teeth gritted, like she's doing her damnedest to be nice and finds her overblown ego extremely bitter to swallow.

Fine. It's the end of the world, anyway. There's no room for silly human pride.

'So, I spoke to your friends,' she spins away on her wheelchair and I fall in step beside her. 'I still don't fully understand it but we're lucky you came when you did. Thank you.'

Huh. That took some guts. 'It was nothing. I didn't do much, to be honest,' I accept her olive branch. 'Eirik and Vidar will keep you safe. They'll fortify this place and help you establish a supply base for the war.'

We move down the hall in silence for a while. 'Before I found this place, a handful of my men stumbled upon something once,' she says. 'It wasn't long after first contact, and we weren't as organized. All we knew was that everything was going to hell and no human logic could explain anything that was happening.'

She looks down at her hands. 'But we found something. It was abnormally bony, and much too large to be human. The skin was thin and almost translucent, stuck in a bizarre way to the body. The worst part was the face—something that resembled the skull of a deer with antlers sprouting from its temples. It was dead.'

My heart constricts. No matter how horrible the wendigos look, they are one of the kindest, gentlest creatures I have ever had the pleasure of meeting. I'm suddenly overcome with longing for Harley's surfing vernacular and Jimmy's fascinating stories about his waterproof boots, and I miss them terribly.

'Common sense and modern science—not to mention all those sci-fi movies—tell us exactly what to do when we encounter such things. Using a scientific approach, we dissect them to analyse them; we figure out what we're up against; or find some evidence that this might be a hoax, a clever conspiracy, and check for surgical seams that prove the creature must be grotesquely man-made somehow. It's the only logical thing to do. Even in their death, that is the most useful thing they can give us.'

Fury burbles up inside me now, ready to burst. 'And what did *you* give them?'

Leslie turns to me and I detect the faintest hint of vulnerability in her steely eyes. 'A proper burial.'

Maybe Leslie isn't so bad, after all.

'This leader. The one with the limp. If those things outside are what he says they are, then their . . . Handler, was it? Their Handler will be even more menacing.'

I nod. 'The Hostiles come from another world, but so do the Ferals,' I tell her, recalling everything Siv and Luna had explained to me when all this began. 'The Hostiles captured the Ferals from one of the planets they colonized, then bred them to be their loyal dogs, trained to wreak havoc on each new planet they invaded. This is usually the first wave—they're set loose to throw everything into chaos before the Hostiles arrive.'

We turn a corner, and some muffled sounds of merrymaking drift into the hallway from a nearby hall.

'These Ferals are basically mindless beasts, and they can only be controlled by a specialized type of Hostile—a bigger, buffer Hostile they call the Handler. They need to be tankier than the average Hostile to withstand Feral bites and accidental attacks. So yeah, these Handlers are hardy, and they won't go down easily.'

Leslie sighs. 'That's . . . comforting.'

'Don't worry. You'll be safe—another batch of defences called the Longma will be here tomorrow, apparently.'

'Thank you.' Leslie shakes her head, incredulous. 'When I was a kid, my brother and I were into all kinds of myths and legends. We thought those creatures were cool and would have given anything to actually meet one of them in real life. Until, of course, I realized none of it was real. I guess I was wrong.' She pauses and then shakes her head again. 'My brother was always the curious one—always with his head in the clouds, while I had my feet firmly on the ground, afraid of ever going up there with him. After one of his travels to the Philippines, he regaled me with stories of this magical bird, this enchanted being, the Ibong Adarna. Something he swore a friend of a friend stumbled upon in the forest once. Legend has it that it would grant you any boon if you passed its test, but if you didn't, well—'

She shrugs and we both stop walking. 'Two so-called adventurers stepped into its lair, a majestic tree that stood in the middle of a clearing, lush and vibrant and bursting with life against the setting sun. Something puzzled them about the ground—all around the tree were oddly shaped rocks, some jagged, some rounded, some jutting upwards from the earth, some lying low on the forest floor almost like they were asleep. The bird hadn't roosted yet, and this one friend opted to lean back against the tree to rest—it had been a long journey and the sun was sinking into the horizon. Plus, there was the faint melody of a birdsong not too far away in the distance, lulling them both into a false sense of security. The other friend volunteered to keep watch, but as soon as the one under the tree shut his eyes, the Ibong Adarna swooped down from the skies in an explosion of rainbow plumage, perched on the branch directly above him—and pooped.'

I bite back a smile. 'You're kidding.'

Leslie's face relaxes. 'It's what my brother said. I think the version of the tale varies from tongue to tongue, but the mythical bird basically pooped on the sleeping man and turned him into stone, and suddenly all those strange rocks under the tree made perfect sense.'

'That's new,' I shove my hands into my pockets. 'Your brother must be quite the storyteller.'

'He was.' Leslie doesn't say anything more, and the past tense weighs heavily on both of us.

I offer her my silence. Now, more than ever, I realize how important it is to work together with everyone, and how, above all else, we should be kind.

That's all we really have left.

After a moment of stillness, she clears her throat and starts heading down the hallway again until we reach the main hall where, just as Leslie had said, a small celebration is taking place. It's hushed and quiet, with candles everywhere illuminating the cosy space, and everyone—all the humans from all walks of life— are allowing themselves this one, small moment of merrymaking and victory, because we hardly ever get these anymore.

But tonight—tonight everyone is all smiles, and no matter what happens tomorrow, we'll at least have this.

Leslie nods her thanks at me, and I nod back, our truce cemented. As she wheels away to join her people, my eyes scan the dimly lit room. I immediately see Didi, waving her Kirby around in excitement among other children she's apparently instantly made friends with, and the Cais are speaking in Cantonese to two other couples on one side of the room. Vidar is still frowning, but he's got a bottle of booze in his hand, and Eirik has a strong arm around his shoulders, beaming from ear to ear. Even Connor is aglow tonight, laughing with Siv, like our earlier conversation didn't just happen, like he didn't just bare his soul to me only to lose a battle against an alien in human flesh who I thought was dead just a few hours ago.

And speaking of Brad . . .

'He's waiting.'

I nearly jump out of my skin as Luna whispers behind my ear. I turn to her and she's holding up a figure-hugging red dress that I would never be caught dead wearing. I remember Aunt

Steph's desperate attempts to slip me into one of these back then for formal events—a cheongsam, I think it's called.

'What's this?'

The manananggal shrugs, a playful, almost giddy, twinkle in her eye. 'It is a surprise. For you. You are to put this on and follow me.'

I gawk in horror at the shimmering thing in all its glamorous glory. 'No freakin' way. You can't make me put that on, Luna. You. Just. Can't.'

* * *

Dammit, Luna.

I reach down and tug at the hemline of the too-tight dress for the nth time, trying to keep the clingy fabric from riding up my body and revealing all the goods. The elegant, floor-length gown is lovely, but it's the long slit on the side that makes me feel like I'm about to flash my crotch with the slightest movement. The fabric wraps around my hips and waist too tightly, and for someone who's never worn a dress like this my whole life, I feel like a Christmas gift.

But Luna took her sweet time picking this out for me, apparently. I don't even know how she managed to find something like this in an abandoned warehouse, but she made such an effort to style this look even though my hair is a mess. It'll be worth it, she said, before shooing me out down this hallway to where Brad is supposedly waiting on the other side of the door.

I sigh. I haven't even showered and there's no way to put on any makeup, so yeah. Some hot date I am.

I shuffle the last few steps in my Chucks and with a final sigh, push open the door to the back exit.

A table for two. It's been ages since I spent a proper night out like this, out in the open, without the constant fear of dismemberment hanging over our heads like the proverbial sword of Damocles. Plastic roses are littered over the ground and some battery-powered tea lights lead a small trail towards the table.

And, of course, there's Brad, standing in a crisp coat and tie and holding out his hand to me.

I slip my hand into his and my breath catches. He takes a moment to look me up and down, then shakes his head.

'Ava, you're . . .' he sighs, 'you're breathtaking.'

I burn up as he draws me close to him and leads me to the table. He pulls up the chair for me and we settle down. I still can't believe that any of this is happening, right when the world is ending.

'So . . . what's all this?'

He flashes that fanged grin at me. 'Our very first date. Just seems a tad unfair that we shouldn't have a proper one, don't you think?'

'But . . . ' I gesture around us. 'How?'

'The Ferals won't be bothering us any time soon, not with the way I . . . handled the matter,' he straightens his tie. 'And as for all this, Luna outdid herself tonight.'

I shake my head in disbelief. Pure joy, sure, but disbelief, nonetheless.

'So,' Brad gestures at the generous spread on the table. Canned corn on plastic utensils and water in wine glasses. 'Quite a feast, yes?'

'Totally. I'm absolutely starving.'

I'm not even kidding. My last proper meal was half a roll of bread and Connor's protein bar, so this actually feels like an all-you-can-eat buffet for me.

Halfway through the meal, I look up and realize Brad's been staring at me this whole time without saying anything. I go red.

'Um. I'm making a complete fool of myself right now, aren't I?'

'On the contrary, you've never looked more beautiful,' he chuckles. 'I just want to . . . I simply can't believe you're here. Really here. With me.'

He reaches over and takes my hand in his. He notices the grimy bracelet and grins. 'You're still wearing it.'

'Of course, I am. I didn't want to give up hope.' I squeeze his hand and he squeezes back. 'Brad . . . how did you find me?'

'There was word among the Avem. They said a small group of elves was protecting a handful of humans, moving from place to place and going against my direct orders to stay put. A female, they say, is safeguarding civilians, stubborn as can be,' he tucks a wayward strand of silver hair—longer now than when I last saw him—behind his ear. 'That's my girl.'

I blush, and he goes on, 'I feared you would hate me, the way we parted. The sudden loss, my weakness, even after your unwavering belief in me at Carl and Edna's. I thought you livid, hopping from place to place, seething. And I said to myself, "way to go, Brad, piss off a woman like that".'

I bite back a smile, and we finish the rest of our meal in silence—the kind of silence that's filled with meaningful nonsense, inside jokes and silly pet names and conversations about fleeting things that won't matter the next day.

It's the kind of silence that isn't silence at all, because if I listened hard enough, I can hear the low hum of our bodies, at the same time, in the same space, connecting with each other even though no words are said.

'Shall we move this to the couch?'

'The couch?' I raise my brows and true enough, a beige couch is right there behind Brad, still with the hefty price tag attached to its side—I've been too mesmerized by this whole dinner date to even notice it.

I laugh. 'Leslie let you drag that thing out here?'

'Let's just say that because I got rid of a Feral infestation for her, she'd do well to grant me a few favours, provided I asked nicely.'

Brad straightens up, sheds his coat and leads me to the couch. He stretches his arms in a bear hug and I snuggle into his body, feeling safe for the first time in a long, long while. He buries his face into my hair and I close my eyes, wishing I can stay like this with him forever.

We stay spooned that way for a while, until he mutters a soft curse under his breath.

'Something wrong?' I look up at him, and he groans.

'Nothing.'

I raise an eyebrow.

'It's just . . .' a tinge of pink stains his cheeks. 'If you don't stop squirming, I cannot promise we'll make it halfway through this night.'

I turn as red as my stupid dress and shift my position to sit beside him instead.

He drapes an arm around my shoulders and stares at me with those crimson vertical slits, a playful smile on his lips. 'So . . . how do first dates work these days? I'm afraid I'm a bit out of touch.'

'I'm not putting out on the first date, if that's what you mean,' I smirk, 'I'm not that kind of girl.'

'Ah. What kind of girl are you, then?'

'The kind that will kick you in the nuts if you try anything funny.'

He chuckles and cups his cheek. 'Of course. The memory of our first kiss is . . . startling, to say the least. I haven't forgotten.'

'Good,' I giggle. 'I'm not opposed to a little make-out sesh, though. You know. If you're into it . . .'

'Hmm. I'm definitely "into it".'

Kissing Brad like this again, I unravel. There's nothing but his scent and his taste and our unbridled, uneven breathing against the stillness of the night. I squeeze my eyes shut even tighter as he moves closer, pinning me against the couch.

He burrows his fingers through my hair and I tug at his tie in desperation, the whole 'not putting out' thing completely out the window, just like that. I move down to kiss his exposed neck and he groans, low and guttural.

'Shh,' I giggle for the millionth time tonight. 'We're not supposed to . . . to be . . .'

'I swear, Ava,' he gasps, 'if you don't sit still, I'm not going to be held responsible for what I might do.'

I swallow.

He traces his fingers against my jaw and runs butterfly kisses against my skin, then he whispers in my ear, 'This isn't your dress, is it?'

'No,' I pant. 'I don't—'

'Good.'

He tugs at the slit against my leg and the fabric rips. I gasp.

'Shh,' he mimics against my ear, smiling. He is such a tease, and I'm annoyed and giddy and crazily addicted to him right now.

He shifts his whole weight on top of me. 'Ava . . . tell me to stop,' he murmurs, 'just tell me to stop.'

But I'm already intoxicated, already in too deep, already too far gone. I can't possibly muster the willpower to stop now.

Which is why, when the door to the back exit slams open with a thud, revealing an extremely apologetic Siv in the doorway, it's the only reason we have to snap back to reality.

Everything that happens next is a blur. Brad straightens his clothes, kisses me on the forehead and excuses himself, just as Luna joins Siv at the door.

She plops down on the couch beside me. I'm still in a daze.

'So,' Luna bites her underlip with the naughtiest look in her eyes. 'How was the date?'

8

Farming

The face of a man.

Fully bearded, with bright, scarlet hair, the face of a man is staring right at me in the tall grass. The lines of his lips contort into a terrifying, almost painful smile, revealing three rows of perfectly sharp teeth.

But that's not even the worst part.

Six feet tall, he pads out of the bushes in broad daylight and stops in front of me. He flexes the scaly, dragon-like wings sprouting from the back of his lion-esque body, and when he folds them back, a scorpion's tail, complete with a spiked tip, swishes carelessly from his rear.

I saw a few of them in the clearing back when I first met Brad—but this, here, now, is my first close-up encounter with an actual manticore. And I'm supposed to ride him.

'*Magandang umaga*, Zahir,' Luna floats by in her bright and strappy sundress and pecks the manticore on his cheek. The twisted smile twists even wider, guaranteeing a couple of nightmares for me over the next few nights. 'We fly today.'

The manticore—Zahir—opens his mouth and screeches in response to Luna in that screeching language that Brad's people have, and both flap their wings in unison before folding them back. Not enough video games in the world could've prepared me for this.

'Zahir likes you,' Luna turns to me. 'A suitable partner for our Harbinger, he says.'

'Um . . . thanks,' I swallow the lump in my throat and fight to keep my heartbeat steady. 'Is it okay to . . . um . . . mount him?'

'A mount worthy of the gods. Zahir will keep you safe,' Luna holds a hand over her heart to drive her point home.

I steal another glance at the manticore's ghastly grin, and somehow I'm still not convinced.

After apologizing like crazy to me last night, Siv explained that the emergency had been a message from the Avem bringing word of a nearby Handler's activities. They believed that one of them is still looking for me with a personal vendetta, six weeks into this invasion.

I'm not surprised. When everything went to hell during first contact, I blew up a truckload of the Ferals' unhatched eggs, and their Handler was livid. It aimed its projectile blades right at me before Brad jumped in between us at the last second. And that was that.

When Connor and I started moving around with Siv and the elf brothers, the Handler couldn't keep tabs on me. But after Brad's terrifying display of power that wiped out all the Ferals prowling around this warehouse last night, the whole affair just couldn't go unnoticed. And then there I was again, pesky little me, smack-dab in the middle of it all, destroying the Handler beacon in the process.

There was a big debate this morning. I wanted Luna to stay behind for Leslie's protection. Siv wanted me to stay behind to keep me safe. Eirik and Vidar wanted to use me as bait to lure the Handler in and get rid of it head-on. Connor wanted me to make myself scarce and stay as far away as possible from this whole mess. And Brad, well, Brad wanted to take me with him.

Brad said I would be safest right beside him, where he can protect me every waking hour of the day. Frankly, I want to leave with Brad too, because my staying here will only endanger everyone else.

Which brings us to this moment, my standing hesitantly in front of this smiling manticore, totally unsure whether I'm going to survive this trip.

Luna is coming with us. We're heading off to recruit these creatures called the Longma and then she's coming right back here to the headquarters to keep everyone safe along with Eirik and Vidar. Then, Brad and I will head out to investigate the Lightbringer sightings in Ming Yu Outpost, and Connor is to leave with Siv to reverse engineer the Handler beacon in Qing Feng Outpost. They won't be alone, as General Wu will be with them. He knows the area best, after all.

And speaking of the general, I honestly didn't expect him to be what he is, because just when I think these creatures couldn't surprise me anymore, something always proves me wrong.

Because the regal General Wu is a Jiangshi—I know that well enough from all of Aunt Steph's stories. Roughly referred to as 'hopping vampires' from Chinese folklore for lack of a better term, the Jiangshi are believed to be reanimated corpses plagued with rigor mortis. I suppose they're sometimes seen by humans in a humourous light, but right now, with his greenish, flaking skin, nonetheless clad in a royal, coat-like robe from the Qing dynasty, General Wu exudes his own brand of leadership that is entirely different from Brad's Harbinger aura. I haven't had the pleasure of meeting him personally—I haven't seen his Longma, either—but I did see him hopping into the checkout area late last night after the festivities.

Yes—hopping.

The talisman taped to the back of his head is a dead giveaway of what he actually is, but even though the Jiangshi are usually portrayed in pop culture with their arms extended, all cartoon-like, I don't think General Wu could ever look ridiculous, no matter what he does. His intimidating vibe is enough to command respect no matter what humans believe.

I spot Connor off to one side and grab the opportunity to excuse myself from Zahir's creepy smile.

Connor looks up from the clipboard one of Leslie's men gave him and sees me approaching.

'Didi wanted me to give you her Kirby, but I told her to hang on to it until you got back,' Connor flashes me a sideways smile. 'Which means you have to promise you'll see her again, and in one piece.'

'Anything for Didi,' I smile back and nod at the clipboard in his hands. 'Do you have any idea what you're doing here?'

'This isn't game design. Plus, there're all sorts of foreign metals and compositions here that aren't even remotely close to our own periodic table of elements,' Connor sighs. 'But tech is tech. I'll just have to see what I can do with it.'

'You have one of the most brilliant minds ever,' I say. 'You'll figure it out, Connor. I know it.'

'I wish I had your faith in my capabilities, but thanks anyway,' he chuckles. 'I'm not taking point here, in any case—I'm just a kid. I'll just try to offer whatever knowledge I have to the real experts over there.'

He gestures to a group of men and women in deep discussion to the far right, and I recognize some of them from when I first barged into their camp. They've been at this since long before we arrived and should hopefully have enough info to make a dent in this war.

Of course, just as Connor and I are looking over, one of them happens to look up and catch our eye—a petite girl who, as fate would have it, looks just about Connor's age. She flips her ebony hair over her shoulders, pushes her glasses up her nose and offers Connor a little wave that's too close for comfort. Connor graciously smiles back, and she actually bites her lip before turning back to her colleagues.

Great. First my feelings about Siv going off on an adventure with him, and now this. I'm not being possessive or anything, and I honestly don't mind Connor moving on and being happy. But I've known him all my life, and he has always been a part of mine. I guess I just . . . don't want to see the whole 'moving on' thing happening right before my eyes.

I suppose he feels the same way about Brad.

Connor clears his throat. 'So, you're really leaving.'

'So are you.'

'I guess we've always had this insatiable desire to head out and save the world. It's what every RPG hero is born to do.'

'That may be true for you, but for me . . . not so much,' I laugh. 'Equip me with some high-level gear and I'll probably be more into it, right?'

Connor doesn't reply. Instead, he lets his gaze linger on my face, and our heart-breaking conversation washes over me in waves. Then he readjusts his glasses and the look on his face is gone.

Of course, the universe picks this exact moment for Brad to walk over to us.

'Connor Brady, is it?' Brad smiles his winning smile. The borrowed coat and tie from last night are gone and he's in a simple grey T-shirt and jeans, but he still looks as gracious as ever. 'Finally. A tremendous pleasure.'

Connor returns the pleasantries. 'The Harbinger.'

'Please. Just Brad,' he shakes his head. 'I admit our first encounter was too uncouth on my part. For that, I apologize.'

'Hey, I didn't know who you were. No biggie.'

Brad runs a sheepish hand through his silver hair. 'You tended to Ava during the initial attack. I cannot thank you enough.'

Connor pauses for a second, and I can actually sense his heart breaking. 'I didn't do it for you.'

Brad's blood-red eyes soften. 'I know.'

All three of us stand there for the briefest of milliseconds without saying anything. I wish I could just rage-quit right now and respawn anywhere else but here.

After what feels like an eternity, Connor holds out his hand to Brad. 'Keep her safe, man.'

Brad returns the firm handshake. 'You have my word.'

Connor stares at Brad for a few more beats, then turns to me with a casual, 'See ya when I see ya.' He heads back into the warehouse, crushing my heart just a little bit more.

Brad tilts his head at me. 'He's taller than me.'

'He's taller than you.'

'I was certain another punch was coming.'

I grin at him. 'Maybe you deserve it.'

'Perhaps I do.'

'For the record, I can take care of myself. On most days. Just don't pitch me one-on-one with a Feral and I'll make it out alive.' I shake my head. 'So if you're done with your little pissing contest, we should probably get going.'

'Pissing contest?' Brad mock-gapes at me. 'Why, there was no such thing.'

I roll my eyes, sling my backpack over my shoulders and march back to where Zahir is standing; Brad follows suit. At the sight of his Harbinger, Zahir kneels with all his four legs to let Brad on. Despite all my hesitation, I take Brad's hand and he pulls me up behind him.

'Hold on to me,' Brad whispers in a low tone, as Zahir rises to his full height and my stomach lurches. I don't need to be told twice.

Eirik and Vidar bow their heads slightly towards Brad, while Siv winks at me. 'See you soon, luv!'

I start to wave goodbye to Siv when Zahir suddenly rears up and I have to grab onto Brad's waist for dear life. Luna flaps her wings beside us and lifts off—clicking and screeching included, reminding me of her horror level each time she flies—and not a second later, Zahir screeches too. He stretches out his own wings and he springs up and we're flying.

We're *flying*.

All those video games and virtual quests have always had me wondering what it would be like, what it would *feel* like, to fly. To feel the wind on my face and the clouds beneath my feet. To soar through the skies and not give a damn about anything. To be absolutely free.

But flying isn't anything like I thought it would be. For one, I can't even open my eyes a decent amount without the wind drying up my eyes and slapping me hard in the face. For another, my arms are clamped in a death grip around Brad's torso because a single slip-up would mean my plummeting to certain death.

There's absolutely nothing liberating about any of this.

All I can hear is Zahir screeching from time to time and Brad screeching back in their language and the mighty flapping of the manticore's wings on either side of me drowning out everything else.

Breakneck speeds and a violent dip later, I feel Brad's welcome hand covering my own and open my eyes to find that we're flying slower now, low and steady enough to afford me a decent look around. Zahir is weaving in and out between tall buildings as quietly as he can, with Luna bringing up the rear.

'Stealth is crucial in the city,' Brad tells me. I'm just glad that Zahir has slowed down enough to allow us to carry on a proper conversation. 'The Ferals and their Handlers cannot reach us when we're too high up, but the humans can. There is no shortage of ammunition they can use against us, heavy artillery or missiles or some such. We've lost quite a few Avem that way. We haven't exactly had sufficient time to differentiate ourselves from the Hostiles, have we?'

And I immediately think that it's just all too unfair, how they're trying to save the world but are being hunted at the same time.

'Our fliers have dwindled greatly in numbers in a mere month's time, slaughtered by the very race we are trying to protect,' Brad goes on, 'which is why summoning the flying Longma to arms is of the utmost importance. But they haven't been responding to my Avem, hence my personal visit.'

As we soar over the dregs of a once-great city, I think about Mrs Gonzales's story, of the Cais dropping off their grandson at the mall and how it exploded just as they were driving away from the kerb. I think of all the humans rioting, the apocalypse parties, the cultists who welcomed the end of the world with open arms and contributed to the havoc as much as they could. I wonder how Brad's people reacted in the face of such overwhelming odds, of fighting off both Ferals and humans, of lashing out in desperation because all they ever wanted was to live in peace in this world. I wonder how many of Brad's men snapped, how many of them were driven to become the monsters they were being made out to be.

A few more minutes of discreet flying later and Zahir starts a slow climb. We've left the city proper and trees are coming into view again, but I can feel Brad's body tensing up. The ascent feels almost too uneventful, like this peace and quiet is a farce, like whatever's at the peak of this mountain isn't something I'd like to find.

And it isn't.

As the fog clears around the summit, everything comes into view all at once.

Carnage. Bits and pieces of creatures—or what were once creatures—are strewn across what's apparently a battlefield, blood and guts caked on the ground to make it impossible to tell what those creatures once were. The shrill, high-pitched roaring of the Ferals is now within earshot, as they charge against herds of horses stampeding against them—only they're not horses at all.

What look like regular horses from afar in both shape and size, actually have thick, reptilian scales in shimmering silver armouring their whole body. Their tails whip around with vigour, long and tapered like that of a rattlesnake. And, instead of a horse's visage, their golden manes silhouette the striking face of a dragon. Although there aren't any tongues of flame spewing from their nostrils, those knife-edged fangs are enough to make them formidable companions in battle.

And then, one of them takes to the skies.

With its impressive wingspan and a mighty roar, the Longma flies up in a rage and dives right down to attack. The feathered wings aren't dragon-esque like Zahir's, but they're fast and efficient and can do a hell of a lot of damage.

But the Ferals have the advantage of size.

Luna screeches and charges. Zahir nosedives to join in the fray; he swings his tail to sting an unwitting Feral in the way. When Zahir eventually lands with a deafening roar, we slide down off him.

Brad turns to me.

His eyes are molten pools of fury. I shoot him a determined look to reassure him that I'll be okay, and it's all the assurance he needs. He leaps at a nearby Feral and drags it down to the ground by its horns, and I turn away before he does something I don't think I'm ready to see.

A long wailing to my right catches my attention. A bloodied Longma is spreadeagled on the ground, its hind legs pinned by a similarly injured Feral looming over it. If the Feral were at a hundred per cent capacity, it could have easily cleaved the injured Longma in two with one swipe of its dangling arms. But, as luck would have it, it's crying out into the sky in pain too. It doesn't have long to live, but it could still bite down on the Longma's exposed neck and sever its head if it wanted to.

My adrenaline kicks in. I make a quick survey of my surroundings—a clear shot, a massive tree to my left, a couple of wobbly edifices directly behind it. I grab the kitchen knife strapped to my thigh and get to work for all the good it's going to do, keeping Siv's training in mind.

Ferals are armoured from top to bottom, but those hard plates are segmented. If you time your strikes right, you can sneak in a hack or two in between the plates, right where their flesh is unprotected, right where it hurts the most. Agility is all I have, so I rush to the hind leg of the Feral and slash.

The high-pitched scream resounds above me. I weave between its legs and make another quick incision on another leg joint, and another, and another. It stomps around and narrowly misses my head, but I keep my eyes trained on the towering tree to my left. My heart thundering in my ears, I make a mad dash to the outsized trunk, positioning myself beneath the tree.

Confused, the Feral has turned its attention from the injured Longma and is now looking for me, infuriated, its horned head lowered to the ground to keep me in its sights. With a deep breath, I take out the dog whistle that I've got on a string around my neck and blow.

The effect is immediate. During first contact, I noticed that the Ferals seemed to be obeying some sort of a soundless command from their Handler, something nobody in our group could hear or understand. So, during one of our raids with Siv, I grabbed a dog whistle from the rack of a looted convenience store, just in case. As an untested hypothesis, it was meant to be used as a last resort, but it seems to be doing its job—and not a very pleasant one at that.

Enraged, the Feral tags me as the source of what's apparently an excruciating sound. It charges.

It snarls and bares its six-inch fangs at me. The inner mouth of humanoid teeth opens just as wide, and the sight almost paralyses my legs.

But at the last second, I leap aside.

The Feral lumbers into the hulking tree trunk, embedding its massive horns into the wood. Splinters explode. It thrashes until its tail ploughs into the ground and bludgeons the two-storeyed structure beside it.

Just as I wanted it to.

The building topples on to the rampaging Feral, and with a final, high-pitched scream of terror, it stops moving.

And I'm left lying there on the ground a few feet from the wreckage, my heart ready to leap out of my throat.

I'm bleeding. The falling debris hadn't been easy to dodge, and I had snagged my leg against the sharp edge of a stray piece of rubble.

I grit my teeth against the pain and stagger towards the Longma still slumped on the ground a few paces from me.

It screeches at me as I approach, but I have no idea what it's trying to say. All I know is that three gashes have split open the silver scales on its hind legs, and I hope against hope that their healing factor is fast enough for it to recover in time.

But before I even have time to catch my breath, another high-pitched scream behind me makes me whip around in dread.

A Feral is staring me in the face, only this one is angrier, scarier and running at full HP with no visible injuries or handicaps. I grip my kitchen knife and adopt my fighting stance—as if my standing between the Feral and the injured Longma will do either me or the Longma any good.

Without giving me enough time to brace for the blow, it lunges.

But almost as soon as its claws leave the ground, an unseen force grabs it by its tail. In one swift motion, Brad wrenches the

Feral away from me and hurls it down the cliff. Now I see how easily he must've thrown that Feral through the warehouse's wall last night.

His silver hair all over his face and a fresh bruise purpling on his cheek, he rushes to me, ignoring the limp I know he's desperately trying to hide. 'Are you hurt?'

Rattled. 'Nothing major,' I hasten to assure him, 'but this one isn't doing so well.'

Brad takes a knee and screeches to the Longma, which screeches right back. He lays a hand on the gashes on its legs and nods. He looks over at me.

'Her name is Qing Shan,' he says, 'and you just saved her life.'

* * *

I tend to the wound on my leg a few minutes later, as I lean against a rock in relief that we survived. The casualties are vast, but the Ferals are gone—at least, for now.

'Their Handler was here,' Brad scowls. 'There are blades on some of the Longma's corpses.'

'The Pure will need time to Bind,' says a grim Luna, hovering a few inches from the ground, the lower half of her body missing. 'There is too much loss here.'

The dust is settling, and what's left of the Longma are pacing around in the rubble. Zahir is resting by the ruins of what appears to have been an ornamental fountain once, nursing his wounds. For the first time, I notice a string of upturned trams tossed aside like toy trains to one side. In the middle of the square, a signboard in Mandarin says something like a station from what little I can understand, only its lights have gone out.

Brad picks up the dead body of an Avem from the wreckage. The corpse is already starting to crumble as they all do when the Pure leaves the Host and finds another to Bind with. But I can still see the steel feathers and the bronze beak.

Brad grits his teeth. 'The fliers aren't enough, I fear. And the Binding, too long a process.' He lays the Avem gently on the ground, bowing his head.

'Our problems grow by the hour, but I can call my sisters to arms,' says Luna. 'It will take time . . .'

'Time we do not have,' Brad's vertical slits of eyes grow darker. 'And if we charge through Japan, there will be much resistance there. We need to pick our battles now and take care not to bite off more than we can chew.'

'Ja . . . pan . . .?'

The disembodied voice startles all three of us. I whip out my knife, while Luna hovers higher off the ground. Even Qing Shan, still sprawled on the ground in front of us, hisses.

Brad steps in front of me protectively. 'Identify yourself.'

'Ja—pan . . .?' The voice repeats. 'Japan?' The sound fades in and out in varying intensity, but in between syllables, I can almost hear the faintest hint of laughter.

The childlike chuckle reverberates above us, and I look up.

Still attached to the tree trunk into which the injured Feral had crashed is a low branch with a single fruit dangling from its tip. The fruit, fresh, ripe and a pinkish peach in colour, is giggling.

Luna flaps her wings higher. 'By the gods . . .!'

'Japan?' the fruit repeats. 'You are from . . . Japan?'

'I am in no mood for games, demon,' Brad clenches his fist. 'Are you friend or foe? Answer quickly; my patience runs thin today.'

'Friend?' the peachy fruit repeats. It stops giggling and turns around.

A humanoid face is smiling at us, a pair of eyes and a nose and a full set of teeth. Brad freezes. The baby-faced fruit scares the crap out of me. I'm used to being the one who's always surprised around here, but if Brad is as startled as I am . . .

'I am . . . friend. Friend from Japan,' the eyes scan the three of us, and then looks at Qing Shan on the ground. The fruit seems to come to its senses then, little by little. 'Longma . . .?'

Brad drops his guard. 'Yes, these are my brethren. How . . .' he frowns. 'Do I know you?'

The fruit stares at him for a long time, and when it blinks, it stops laughing. 'Harbinger? Harbinger.'

Brad screeches in an attempt to communicate, but it shakes its fruity head, then mumbles something in what sounds like Japanese. 'I . . . cannot. Do not . . . remember.'

'*Kapatid*,' Luna lays a gentle hand on the branch. 'What has befallen you?'

'I am . . . Japan. Japan,' the fruit struggles. 'I am . . . Jinmenju. From Japan.'

'The Jinmenju,' I gasp. 'Aunt Steph told me about them.'

Brad raises an eyebrow at me.

'Legends tell of trees from China that bear fruit shaped like human heads. Demons in the woods that look like laughing babies. The "Human-Faced Tree". The Jinmenju,' I say. 'They're said to originate from the mainland, but its seeds have been dispersed everywhere, reaching as far as Japan and even some parts of Southeast Asia.'

'How have I never heard of this tale?'

'They're extremely rare. There used to be gardens and gardens of Jinmenju, but it's been said that humans have eaten them all, some say for immortality, some for power. It's fuzzy,' I shrug, shaking my head. 'I can't believe Aunt Steph was right.'

'I . . . am remembering,' the Jinmenju speaks. 'The Pure. The Binding. The Lightbringer.' It stares at Brad, 'and you, Harbinger. The Watcher on Distant Shore.'

'How is this possible?' Brad shakes his head. 'I should know every single thing about my people. I can't believe . . .'

'It is . . . rare. For Jinmenju to regain its senses. As the Pure . . . we Bind with plants. We know not any better. And we . . . become one with Nature. Become one with the trees. And then we forget . . .' the Jinmenju giggles, then shakes its head, 'we forget.'

'You mean there's more of you? Countless?' I pipe in. 'All the Pure who inadvertently Bind with plants become Jinmenju, and over time, you just . . . forget to be sentient?'

'Yes, human girl,' the Jinmenju smiles at me. Its giggles tinkle in the air like wind chimes. 'The Paladin. The kitsune. She made mention of you. I remember.'

'Kiyoshi was here?' I stand up straighter. 'Where is she now? What happened? Did you speak to her?'

'The Jinmenju . . . do not speak. We watch. We observe. We know everything, see everything. We are all connected . . .' it chuckles. 'Peace. Freedom. Joy. The mother of life . . . this Earth. We are all connected.'

'We are caught in a war, brother. The Hostiles have committed all manner of atrocities against this planet, much like they did ours. Please,' Brad says, 'if you have eyes everywhere, we need you to come back into the fold. We need to win this war, and I daresay you'll greatly tip the scales in our favour.'

'War . . . is destruction. It is destruction of all life. And we are all connected . . . connected in this life.' The Jinmenju stops smiling. 'You are tainted, Harbinger. You have let power corrupt you. Like the Lightbringer . . . like the Lightbringer. You will be driven mad.'

Brad goes pale. 'The Lightbringer . . . you've seen him?'

'A bird. A turtle. A tiger. A dragon. He is ever-changing . . . ever-evolving. He has led both hope and ruin for the Pure here.' The Jinmenju lets out a small chuckle, then stops itself. 'If you seek him, you only seek death.'

Brad lowers his head then, unable to say anything else. The shock of knowing that the Lightbringer, his noble leader and the greatest of them all, is truly alive somewhere must be too much for him to take.

So I speak up. 'Where is he now?'

The Jinmenju turns to me. 'In the land of the wingless dragon . . . the four-god bows its head in shame. Human girl, human girl.' It contorts its face into a taut smile, then retracts the grin. 'I see all . . . there is power for you there.'

My jaw drops. *What?*

The silence stretches on until the Jinmenju starts giggling again, its sinister yet sad laughter echoing through the emptiness. Qing Shan wobbles up from the ground, flapping her wings and hissing at the tree.

The Jinmenju turns to her. 'Longma, I mourn for your loss. The metals three . . . they keep you there. Trap you. The Pure can no longer Bind.'

'New technology? From the Hostiles?' Luna gasps. 'But how? How could they possibly know . . .'

Brad absently runs a hand over his own torso, at the scars that the magnetized blades bore into him underneath his shirt. 'So, once we are hit and die, we stay dead.'

'Watcher on . . . Distant Shore . . .' the Jinmenju struggles to speak, giggling more violently between a few Japanese words. 'I wish you well. I am . . . friend. Japan. I . . . forget. Forget. Mother . . . is calling . . .'

Like it's being wiped off, the humanoid face on the peachy fruit fades until all that's left is the faint echo of its laughter, giggling and giggling until the fruit trembles and falls to the ground. I reach down to pick it up.

There's nothing there.

9

World Map

'That totally makes no sense,' I dig up a bottle of water from the wreckage and shove it into my backpack. 'How would the Hostiles even know to develop tech like that? They have no idea that you guys have built a life here over the centuries. They're supposed to be clueless about the Binding, right?'

'They're certainly well-informed, and I have no idea how.' Brad runs a hand through his hair and sighs. 'If the magnetized blades are truly permanent, then our advantage in numbers is lost.'

'The tree. I fear it speaks the truth,' Luna is staring at the remnants of a reception desk in front of her. 'The bodies of the Longma struck with the blades—they are not disappearing.'

'Then death is certain,' Brad rubs his temples. 'Impeccable timing.'

I crouch and rummage through the debris some more, leaving them to their thoughts. Qing Shan bends her dragon-neck down and sweeps her huge nostrils across the ground to help me search. She hasn't left my side since she recovered.

We've moved the conversation into this structure precisely because I wanted to see if I could find some salvageable goods, and I'm right. We're inside the ruins of what appears to have been some sort of a tourists' souvenir shop, and despite the utter devastation in this place, some of the mannequins are actually still standing.

'At any rate, what's done is done,' Brad absently picks at his stubble. 'We cannot afford to falter here. We dispatch what's left of the Avem to spread this news at once.'

'*Pero* . . . the Lightbringer,' Luna sounds apprehensive. 'The news doesn't trouble you?'

'If he is truly alive, I . . .' Brad looks down, 'I wish to see him. To know what madness found him there.'

'Then let's go look for him,' I step towards them. 'The Jinmenju says it's from Japan, so we should probably just ask Kiyoshi. Where is she, anyway?'

'She is preoccupied with the European border—everyone has their own role in this war. But she knows nothing of this. As Paladins, she and Athanasios would have been the first to have searched far and wide for the Lightbringer only to find themselves disappointment,' Brad says. 'But perhaps there was some truth to the Jinmenju's babblings.'

The Paladins were the Lightbringer's fiercest generals back on their home planet, but Kiyoshi and Athanasios—I know him better as Ethan—are the only ones left. If the Lightbringer wanted to be found, then the telepathic nine-tailed fox and the Sudoku-loving centaur would have found him by now.

'Then I bring the Longma back. To the humans. Strength and valour . . . the Longma are not wanting. The humans will be in good company,' Luna unfurls her wings behind her. 'And then you will permit me to call my sisters?'

'Fly where you must, Luna. There is hope for us yet.'

Luna nods, smiles at me, then stretches out her arms for a quick embrace. 'Be safe, *hija. Hanggang sa muli.*'

I give her a little squeeze, hoping against hope that I'll get to see her again soon. And with a small wave, she drifts out of the visitor centre. I hear her screeching outside as the Longma screech back, and moments later, in a whoosh of wings swirling and flapping in unison, they're gone.

'Quite the exit,' Brad stares out the door. 'But there's no time to waste. I'd much rather find the Lightbringer and have him lead us into battle again in the shortest time possible.'

'Cool,' I zip up my backpack. 'If we find your Lightbringer again—*when* we find him—we'll win?'

'I should hope so, but there it is, isn't it? That blind hope. Perhaps talking about it diminishes it somehow, makes it less real,' Brad sighs. 'For now, though, it's ours—and I pray you'll indulge my quiddities for a little while longer.'

* * *

I keep my arms wound tight around Qing Shan's neck as we soar through the skies in the dark. Zahir speeds behind us—his massive wingspan and body size make him slower than Qing Shan by comparison. I can't exactly see where we're headed, but I'm thankful these two know precisely where to go.

I open my eyes a tad to sneak a glance at Brad riding Zahir. Even though we've been travelling for a couple of hours now, slowing down in the cities and speeding up in less populated areas, he hasn't spoken a word in all this time.

He's worried. I know he is. Before all of this went down, he had a clear moment of weakness one night, breaking down and believing he wasn't good enough to lead his people to victory. I have never seen him as vulnerable as he was that night. Even though we worked out his issues and he's been playing his role well so far, I know that there are still some insecurities inside that brave exterior, gnawing at him from the inside.

And now that there's even the slightest possibility that the Lightbringer might be alive, he's clinging to that tiny sliver of hope as best he can.

Luna should be back at the warehouse by now. She would've already told Leslie how to work with the Longma to help defend their stronghold, and would have explained about the Hostiles' new tech with the magnetized blades. They would've sent out the Avem to spread the word, and Connor, I'm hoping, has probably landed where he should and has made some progress on deciphering the Handler's beacon.

Supply bases are being set up around the world. Brad's people—Ethan and the chupacabra and the banshees and the Pure and all the creatures I haven't even met yet—would've set up camps, prepping defences, fending off Ferals and saving human refugees. The Hostiles might have taken the human race by surprise during first contact, but we're catching up. I know we are—I *have to believe* we are.

Which means Brad is doing okay so far. I've been trying to encourage him as much as I can—after all, he's been doing the same for me ever since I met him, believing in me and in my capabilities even when my self-esteem and self-confidence levels were at an all-time low. Without any supernatural abilities of my own, empowering and enabling him is the least I can do to help him be a better leader—all I have is my faith in him.

Still, despite all this, Brad's faith in his own work just doesn't seem to be enough. So if finding the Lightbringer is going to lighten the burden of responsibility on his shoulders, not to mention grant me that 'power' thing the Jinmenju was talking about . . .

. . . then it's definitely worth the risk.

As I mull over that last thought, an abrupt screech from Zahir makes me whip around.

In the darkness, I can almost make out what seems to be a long metal beam protruding from Zahir's wing. He's swerving and Brad's screeching with him and I try to steer Qing Shan towards them but then my own Longma roars in pain.

And we're falling.

The wind and the speed and the sharp, sharp pain and I've somehow landed on a netted hammock of sorts, dangling just a few inches off the ground. My mouth is wide open in a scream I can't hear before my vision blurs.

I can smell blood, around me, from me, somewhere. Footsteps scurry around and all I can see are towering trees in the moonlight. Frantic words fade in and out of focus. Just when I feel the last of my strength ebbing away, I see what appears to be long, hairy, spindly things creep out from the shadows—colossal, pointy and weird. I must be losing it because those things actually look like . . .

. . . a giant spider's legs.

And I realize just what kind of a 'hammock' I'm lying on.

Screams. Around me. Human. Panicked voices, footsteps scrambling away. All I remember is a woman peering down at me before everything fades to black.

* * *

The lights in my room flicker as my father pounds a fist on the dining table downstairs on his way out. The Pure are watching and Aunt Steph is crying but no, it's Cassie, her mascara running in ominous black trickles down her cheeks. Roy is driving the Jeep but he's shrieking now, the last sound he'll ever make, as the weight of Marcello's roof proves too much for his frail human body. Ethan is playing Sudoku with me, but the grids are bones from a chupacabra's carcass beside him, and Kiyoshi is in her nine-tailed-fox form prancing around with unconscious human mercenaries in a macabre dance.

The mayor of Canyon Falls is giving his speech about human advancement and cutting up Brad's people during my graduation ceremony and Jimmy is the guest speaker and he takes the stage and faces us all and his stomach is gaping open, mice scraping and clawing and eating away at his guts in a glorious display of blood and innards.

Big Bad Wolf steps up to the podium, but he's rotting, decomposing, three magnetized blades jutting out from his torso like badges of honour.

'Happy graduation, Ava,' he grins at me and I toss my hat into the air, but it's heavy, so heavy; I can't move my arms, my body is frozen solid; now I'm pinned under the roof of Marcello's too and there's nowhere to go.

I wake up.

I'm in a cave. A dark cavern littered with lit candles, the place should make me feel claustrophobic. But something about the ambience keeps the atmosphere warm and intimate instead, like the only thing missing is some fluffy socks and a soothing cup of hot tea.

I'm lying on a pile of blankets. The nightmare clutches at my reality as if unwilling to let go, but the blankets provide a rare luxury I haven't had in a long while. Something in the air smells good—and my stomach rumbles out loud.

'You're up!' A smiling woman with fair skin and narrowed eyes is watching over me. Her dark curls cascade over her shoulders like a black waterfall and continue further downwards to provide a demure cover over her naked chest. Two voluptuous mounds hide behind those jet-black tresses, and she grins down at me.

'I know you have questions, but you should save your strength. I barely had enough time to spin that web to catch your fall, you know,' she says. 'Don't worry; you're safe here. My name is Izanami and I am a Jorogumo—or at least, they say I am.'

Joro-what? I struggle to sit up and she reaches across to help me.

Below her perfectly petite waist is the round, hairy abdomen of a spider—from the sides sprout eight long legs, stretched out menacingly across the cave floor.

I should've promptly gone into cardiac arrest, but both my body and my brain are too tired to react.

'The humans who attacked you, they just didn't know any better, you know? Just harpooning everything and figuring out what's what after. Can't exactly blame them—the world's gone cuckoo,' Izanami shrugs, her curls shifting across her smooth shoulders. 'Qing Shan and Zahir will be fine. They just need a while to let their wings recover fully, that's all.'

'Where . . .' I wince, 'where's Brad?'

'He's in the living room,' Izanami grins. 'Of course. Brad. I should've led with that. He's your lover, right?'

I can feel the hot blush burning my face.

She waves her hand. 'No need to be modest around here. Pietro and I are all about reckless abandon. You know, seizing the day and all that? Living life to the fullest? Just because we can't have kids, doesn't mean we can't have a little fun, right?'

I go even redder if that were even possible. 'I—he— we're not—'

'I'll give you some pointers,' she winks. 'Pietro oughta teach the Harbinger a thing or two, too, come to think of it. My husband knows *all* the moves. If he ever comes home, that is.'

I'm totally dying.

'I'm almost done with your meal. You look like you haven't eaten anything in a year.' Her spider legs raise her up to her full gargantuan height. 'Take it easy here for a bit, will you? I'll be back in a sec.' She scuttles away through the passageway of the tunnel to my left and disappears.

As soon as I feel like I've pulled myself together, I take a deep breath and follow after her.

The corridor leads into another candle-lit chamber, the flickering light casting everything in an otherworldly glow. There's makeshift furniture here, a wooden bench and a table haphazardly pieced together from rocks. Brad is leaning against the stone counter with his back to me, mumbling to himself, while inspecting something in his hand shielded from my view.

'Spare me your theatrics,' Brad growls to himself, 'you couldn't even catch a cold if you tried.'

I clear my throat and he turns around, a tint of pink staining his cheeks. He shoves the thing in his hand behind him, which I can see is a sheet of paper. He straightens up. 'Ava, how are you feeling?'

'A little woozy, but nothing I can't shake off, thanks to Izanami,' I smile. 'Are you okay? Qing Shan? Zahir?'

'A day or two in the den should do them some good. Nothing they can't shake off, as you so succinctly put it.' He leans over and plants a quick peck on my cheek, but even that's enough to melt the icy coldness in my hands and feet.

'A day or two of breathing room then, I guess?'

'If only things were that simple,' Brad sighs and hands me the document he was holding behind his back.

I frown. 'It's . . . a medical certificate?'

'Izanami's husband apparently thinks he has a rare physiological condition and that he's *dying*,' Brad stresses the last word and rolls his eyes, his voice dripping with sarcasm. 'Now, it appears he has wandered off to indulge in his eccentricities, but while he usually pops back after a few days, it has now been a week since he disappeared.'

'And?'

'. . . and I've promised Izanami I would look for her husband, as a thank-you for taking us in. So . . .' Brad sighs and pockets the medical certificate, 'while Qing Shan and Zahir recover in the den, I'll be making the fullest use of my faculties to look for my wayward brother . . . against every fibre of my being.'

I raise an eyebrow at him. 'Your brother?'

'Not in the literal sense, but Pietro is . . . like me. And I hate that guy.' Brad grits his teeth. 'I'll go only with your permission, of course, and only if you'll permit me to take you along. Those six weeks of separation maimed me, Ava.'

I almost reach out to cup Brad's cheek in response, when Izanami pops in from a tunnel to my left.

'Good—you're both here,' she scuttles forward and smiles at me. 'Dinner's ready.'

10

Quality-Of-Life Update

A tuft of black fur brushes past me to my right and my spine tingles. Izanami has been scuttling beside me for hours now, but I don't think I'll ever get used to the giant spider hovering in my periphery. Each time the silhouette of her hairy belly shifts, I feel an instinctive jolt shudder through me—I have to constantly remind myself that I'm not about to be mauled to death by a gigantic arachnid.

We have to travel on foot now, she says, as the locals who shot us down are still on the lookout for creatures they can drag down from the sky. Because they know they're no match for the Ferals on the ground, they've apparently taken it upon themselves to target the heavens instead—not knowing, of course, that the monsters below are nothing like the monsters overhead.

'Pietro can take care of himself,' Brad gritted out through his teeth before we left Izanami's cave. 'Why should this absence be any different from his previous truancies?'

'Call it a hunch. Or fate—whatever you want to believe these days,' Izanami shrugged. 'We do this dance where we flit away from each other and bounce right back together like we're at the ends of an elastic string. But this just feels . . . weird somehow. Plus, you guys happened to drop by, right? Literally. So, I figured, who better to help me than the Harbinger himself?'

Brad heaved a resigned sigh then, and we set off to the nearby human campsite that Izanami thinks is holding Pietro captive somehow. She had scouted the area before, but there were apparently too many armed humans for her to just barge in unannounced. She swears Pietro is being held prisoner inside one of their tents for some reason, which brings us to where we are right now: crouched behind what looks like an old candy store, the colours that once brought it to life now dull and fading.

We haven't seen a single soul in sight and I hate to even dwell on how the town was emptied out this way—whether the inhabitants chose to leave or were simply . . . eaten.

I shake the image out of my head and try to focus instead on the scene before me: in the middle of the abandoned town is a human encampment barricaded with barbed wires and sandbags that are obviously telling us to stay the hell away. Armed men stand guard by the entrance of the camp, and from what I can squint at inside, there seem to be rows of tents filled with . . . whatever it is these men are guarding.

The camp looks odd and out of place here, occupying the middle of an empty town, mushrooming like an unwanted overgrowth from the earth. Everything is thrown together in a desperate bid to appear intimidating—even the men standing guard look pieced in a hurry, a patch of fear and a patch of feigned bravery and a patch of hopelessness, stitched side by side and sewn in place because there's nowhere else to go, no one else to call, nothing else to do but put up a front when the world is coming to an end.

'When faced with oblivion, there's no limit to what a desperate man fighting for survival will be forced to do,' Brad had told me once, before I joined his ragtag team of mythological misfits, before he and I found . . . something in each other. 'The world never fails to come up with more ingenious ways to kill with each new day.'

I guess that's never been truer than now.

'So, what's the game plan here?' I whisper. 'These men don't exactly look friendly.'

'The guards work on shifts,' Izanami gestures down to her furry belly. 'I obviously can't sneak in like you both can, but I'll happily provide firepower cover for you when the shit hits the fan.'

'Assuring,' Brad sighs for the millionth time. 'Not a friendly lot—that much is true.'

'Sorry, Harbinger.'

He shakes his head. 'It's not that I don't *want* to do this for you, Izanami. It's the person I'm saving I'm not too fond of.' He gives the guards stationed out front another once-over, then turns to me. 'Well, then.'

I nod, and we both sneak over to the last torn-down wall we can hide behind before we actually have to march up to the camp entrance. I glance back behind me and see Izanami in her place, still behind the candy shop, grinning at me with a thumbs-up sign. She does look a bit ridiculous—this horrific, half-spider, half-woman creature towering behind a candy stall with absolutely no clothes on. I take a mental screenshot of this very moment and save it in my mind's archives, just so I can pull it back up when I need a pick-me-up in the near future. I have a sinking feeling that I'll need it sooner than later.

A short, scrawny man with a perpetual stoop saunters out of the camp and starts barking instructions to the two guards out front. He seems to be the leader of the group despite his small stature, given his confident attitude. He pushes his glasses up the bridge of his nose, sneers one last time at the guards and strides into the tent in a huff. The chastised guards start back into the camp to end their shift just as Izanami had predicted, but not before exchanging grimaces, most likely at Sneery Glasses Guy's expense.

'Our unwavering window awaits,' Brad smirks at me. 'Let's be off then, shall we?'

Without another word, we do a crouched run to the entrance and slip into the campsite. Brad winks at me and we split up, moving behind anything we can use as cover. It almost feels hilarious to be doing this in real life when I've spent countless hours on stealth video games avoiding the guards' conveniently placed cones of vision that may or may not turn red when they start getting suspicious.

Obviously, there are no visible cones to avoid now, no gullible AI or non-player characters who often confuse my sneaking around with a passing breeze—just the very real danger of getting caught and quite literally losing my head.

But this is exactly what I've been doing for the past several weeks with Siv—sneaking in and out of places to scavenge for food or search for survivors. Some days, we slip in and out of these makeshift camps undetected. Most days, we leave empty-handed—on worse days, we leave with one person short.

As expected, there are two rows of tents within the camp. A few more guards loiter about here and there—the vibe isn't as intimidating as Leslie's warehouse, but it does seem unlikely that a camp like this might be harbouring an alien fugitive who apparently hasn't got long to live.

With an unspoken mutual agreement, Brad takes one of the rows of tents while I take the other. Taking a deep breath—scanning around first to make sure no one is around—I step into the first tent.

What I see inside never would've been something I could've been prepared for, however bizarre things have been over the past few weeks.

Two imposing steel cages stand before me in the dark. The bars have seen some physical abuse, a nick in one corner and a bend in another. There are marks everywhere—scratches, maybe teeth, or something that desperately tried to claw its way out of captivity. While the flimsy sandbags protecting the camp don't look too formidable in themselves when push came to shove, these cages obviously took priority when the humans were building their little fortress. Whatever was inside must've been more important to keep safe—or way more dangerous to let loose.

True enough, something sensed my presence the moment I stepped into the tent. Beyond the pitch-black of the first cage, two golden orbs turn in my direction, hovering closer and closer until I can make out a figure with what little light is filtering through the tent's door flap.

Behind the steel bars is a leopard—amber eyes, curious yet seething, as a low growl emanates through its bared fangs. It locks its gaze with mine and tilts its head, and that's when I see it—a single horn protruding from the middle of its forehead, a bloodied tip trembling in anticipation of its next victim.

Which, hopefully, isn't me.

I stand there frozen in both fear and wonder, just as a second creature in the neighbouring cage pads forward to get a closer look at me. When it moves as far as the steel bars will let it, something slithers behind it. The creature's tails swish through the black air—all five of them.

I realize then that these two magnificent beings must be Brad's people too, captured and tortured and either kept here as toys or used as weapons. My second hunch, it seems, is closer to the truth—both leopard-like creatures have deep scars carved into their faces and torsos, dried blood caked in their fur. The amber gazes bore deeper into my eyes, unflinching, unwavering. Angry, sad, alone.

I may not be able to screech their language the way Brad and the others can, but this, right here—this white noise between us, this mutual helplessness in the face of a doomed world . . . it's more than enough.

I extend my hand towards the cage, but the sudden movement makes both creatures flinch—and it breaks my heart. No horns or growls or claws or talons or fangs can diminish the horrors that these two beasts have experienced in captivity.

So, against my better judgement, I grab hold of the metal bars on the cage.

And set them free.

For a split second, I imagine them pouncing and me wishing for a quick and painless death, and the guards will rush in and Izanami will never find her husband and the last thing I'll see is the horror on Brad's face when he sees the carnage.

But nothing of the sort happens. Instead, something swells inside me—something hard and heavy in my chest, threatening to balloon up and burst with empathy at the way the two leopards are eyeing me, padding out of their cages and leering down at me with confusion and rage and still so, so lonely. A different kind of strength surges through me now, how I can communicate with these creatures with just a look, how my heart speaks to theirs and how I've always known how to read their eyes, the way I saw past the alien bravado in Brad's when we first met and witnessed his sadness from within.

Is this it, then? What the Jinmenju was talking about? That power, that strength? Is it power that's not power in the literal sense; the strength to find humanity where there's none; the courage to follow my heart when the world screams at me to do the opposite? Is this the only reason I'm here? The only reason I'm still alive? Because I've always seen past the superficial appearances and the myths and the monsters and discovered the reality of what's within?

It takes one more second of all three of us staring at each other before one of the creatures makes a sound. It launches its horn into the air and roars, and in the next second, both creatures leap out of the tent into the madness outside.

And the fire burns.

I dash out of the tent to find the two creatures on a maniacal rampage and the men shooting at everything in sight in their panic, Izanami's husband nowhere to be found. Even Sneery Glasses Guy is waving his arms around in the middle of the field like he's trying to take flight for all the good it'll do. I duck down just as a rogue bullet zips by my head, and when I crawl my way behind a crate, I see Brad sprinting towards me through the haze of the gunfire.

He drops down and shields me with his body, his breath warm in my ear. 'What happened to "tread lightly"?'

'Sorry,' I wince as more bullets whiz past us. 'I couldn't just leave them there—'

'I know. I'm glad you didn't,' Brad helps me up and wraps an arm around me. 'Let's move.'

We dodge the small fires on the ground—Brad's limp less noticeable now—and rush to a nearby structure just as an explosion far to our right rips through the night. It's far enough to keep us safe, but it still leaves my eyes ringing. I cringe.

In the fog of the firefight, I see the silhouette of a giant spider putting the men in their place in the midst of the battle, just as Brad raises his voice over the din of the chaos. 'The Zheng need help. I'm going to—'

I never do find out what Brad says next, because an empathic boom wrenches away my attention. Somewhere to my left, the haze clears. A man steps out of the shadows to join the fight, leaping into the fray with the speed and strength that I've only ever seen Brad possess . . . which can only mean one thing.

'For heavens' sake,' Brad groans beside me, then, straightening up, he promptly plunges into the scuffle himself.

I know I should be in the thick of battle too with whatever little fighting skills I have at my command, but I just can't tear my eyes away from the newcomer no matter how hard I try.

Because he's completely naked, and I'm physically unable to do anything but gawk at him.

* * *

'So, Pietro is . . . '

'Like me, yes,' Brad is still fuming, even after we've cleaned ourselves up and are now back in Izanami's burrow. She was kind enough to prepare a room-slash-cavern hole for Brad and me, while she and her husband . . . sorted things out. 'He is the worst.'

'Huh.'

Brad glances at me, a sceptical look in his crimson eyes. 'What's that supposed to mean?'

'What?'

'That sound you just made,' he clenches his jaw and I notice just how much his stubble has grown since the last time I saw him. 'And don't think I haven't noticed you've been asking about Pietro all night.'

I bite back a smile. 'Are you jealous?'

'No,' he blushes, which isn't something you see every day. 'I just . . . I hate that guy.'

I inch closer to him on the blanket we're on and snake my arms around his neck. I nibble on his lower lip until his eyes flutter shut and he releases a soft, pleasured breath.

I draw back. 'Happy now?'

He sighs. 'You should do that more often.'

'You should shave.'

'There are more pressing matters. . .' he tugs me closer.

I giggle and gently push him back. 'Focus. We need to leave bright and early tomorrow, remember?'

'Right.'

When Brad and the others subdued the humans in the camp, the two leopard thingies—the Zheng—gave me one last lonely stare before they disappeared into the distance. I can't bear to even think of the tortures they must've endured, what it must've felt like to be held captive, beaten into submission and used as subservient weapons, so much so that they've forgotten who they once were, of the proud alien race to which they belonged and shared with Brad and the rest. I could sense their frustration and hopelessness of having lost everything, including their language, how maddening it must feel not knowing where to go from here.

After they left, Pietro introduced himself to me, shining silver hair that mirrored Brad's cascading down his chiselled shoulders. I gaped as world-class pecs and rock-hard abs straight out of a Photoshopped poster stared right back at me.

'How lovely,' he grinned at me with a perfect set of teeth behind perfectly puckered lips and the smoothest jawline ever. 'A pleasure, Ava. My name is Pietro.'

I had expected Izanami's husband to share her arachnid features, but Pietro was . . . all man. Buff and muscular and just too good to be true. Pietro was totally, completely, irreversibly naked, showing off the goods in all their glory.

I averted my eyes and forced myself to stare straight ahead at his face, which was just as distracting. The piercing red eyes twinkled at me.

'Oh, please.' Brad grumbled. 'Throw something on, would you?'

'Edgy, aren't we?' Pietro chuckled. 'This is how we're meant to live, Brad. Life is short—too short to be shackled by inhibitions.'

'For the last time,' Brad gritted his teeth, 'you are *not* dying of this imaginary medical condition you so adamantly believe you have.'

Pietro shook the long curls on his head. 'Aren't I, now? You would do well to appreciate what life gives you, Harbinger. You've had centuries, yes, but you never know when you might breathe your last.'

Brad muttered something rude under his breath and I could actually feel him fuming beside me.

'Um, so,' I tried my best to keep my gaze levelled with Pietro's face, 'you're Izanami's husband.'

'We cohabit, yes, but more like lovers,' Pietro looked me up and down and my heart began to beat faster. 'I can see why Brad is enthralled. You are exquisite.'

I opened my mouth to speak, but nothing came out. Brad wrapped an arm around my shoulders and leered.

'Don't get any ideas.'

Brad kept his arm around me all the way back to Izanami's lair as she and Pietro discussed the terms of their latest relationship experiment. Pietro had apparently gallivanted off somewhere and wasn't even in the camp we had just destroyed. When he heard all the commotion, he came over to see what the fuss was all about. He had been having fun—too much fun—on his own with who-knows-what doing whatever his fantasies desired and conveniently forgot to come home for a full week.

Naturally, Izanami had just as much liberty to do the same in their strange open marriage. I'll never get my head around how such a relationship worked.

'You should get some rest,' Brad jolts me out of my reverie. 'I'll keep watch tonight.'

'You should let Pietro do that.'

The chiselled jawline hardens. 'Absolutely not.'

And I remember how he mentioned a 'brother' who walks around stark naked all day, six weeks ago when we were leaving Carl and Edna's B&B. He did say he hated that guy with all his guts.

Carl and Edna. My heart aches at the memory of the sweetest couple in the world, who took us in when we were lost and gave us the warm welcome we were desperate for that day in the forest. How we spent the next few days oblivious to the world, how one selfish decision could've given me the life I'd always wanted in the self-contained universe of us.

Did they survive first contact, I wonder? Did Carl make it out of the rubble alive, safe and warm as they had made us feel when we sought them out? Or did Edna hold on to her husband one last time, as the monsters and sheer hopelessness closed in on them?

I think back on all the people in that town, how it wasn't just Canyon Falls that counted its days in fading sunsets, how mothers lost their daughters and fathers lost their sons. The nameless passers-by and the faceless streets, the regulars at Marcello's and Annie in London, Aunt Steph at her desk and even the mayor in his office.

I remember reading an article about Dr Lois Tonkin once, who said that while we always believe that grief shrinks over time, the reality is that the grief actually stays the same—it's our life that grows bigger around it. I can't help but wonder how that concept applies to humankind now, when all that's left for us to move on in our lives is more death around us.

And it's that chasm in my chest that makes me realize I haven't even asked Brad how he's doing—really doing—since everything fell apart.

I reach out to hold his hand. 'Brad, are you . . . okay?'

His vertical slits flick over at me, but I've learnt to see beyond the alien eyes now, past the tenacity, past the shame. He looks away.

'I'm . . . fighting. On most days, it's for you. The "voice in the battlefield", Ava of the violent video games, Ava of the fiery pixelated sky.' He tries to sneak a smirk at me, but the smile is fleeting on his lips. 'On other days, it's for the Pure, but once or twice something creeps in and it's for me. Brad of the lonely bookshelves and the forgotten dreams. Brad of the endless waiting and not knowing what he's waiting for.'

He squeezes my hand. 'In this long and winding life, there were countless times I tried to hold on to the memory of the people who mattered to me, their faces, and their smiles and their voices, but they fade away—they all do. I tried to immortalize them in my heart instead, but time takes them away, cruel and finite. And all that's left is me, still struggling to remember the exact moment the world moved on and left me behind.'

It hits me then, how desperate I was to keep moving, keep going, keep rushing forward when the Hostiles attacked. How Cassie left and all I could grab onto was her Hello Kitty watch, how Roy was crushed under the debris of the levelled Marcellos', his dad suffocating in the dark with him. How they never got to see the monsters outside, and were they luckier then? Was it better never having seen the horrors of the night? Did Roy dream of all the sundaes we had and the laughter we shared and never once wondered how life would've turned out otherwise?

And did Cassie, beautiful, bubbly, loyal Cassie, lose her zeal and her light and her shine, all her plans for college crumbling in front of her, the love of her life buried under their failed dreams and her best friend leaving with her only brother? Is she going through heartbreak now, the heartbreak of trying to forget, or the heartbreak of trying to remember?

There were days when I tried to talk to her in an abandoned house or a looted store when we were on the run, but the empty room would sigh back at me. I always thought that I had gotten over being shackled by my past now, that I'm no longer wearing the 'orphan girl' badge on my chest like a scarlet letter, no longer shrouded by this veil of sadness about my Mom's death, no longer looking for my father with this sense of abandonment as the only thing he left behind. I always thought that I had accepted all of that and moved on to a brand new me.

But I guess, that no matter how much I justified my leaving and embarking on this impossible quest, one thing still haunts me with glaring, unforgiving finality—that when I left for this adventure to save the world, I left my best friend too.

The crumpled letter burns a hole in my pocket and in my heart—a reminder of the guilt that I carry around with me wherever I go.

'Madness, isn't it? This thing called hindsight?' Brad whispers. 'We spend our whole lives trying to live without regrets, yet in the end we always find that we never actually lived at all.'

11

Secret Character

'They're kinda like parasites, if you think about it,' Izanami pouts as we sneak through another abandoned town the next day. We crouch down in the backyard of what was once somebody's home—I can just about make out a tiny dog kennel to one side. This seems to be the trend nowadays—cities evacuated in a hurry, plates uncleared and jobs unfulfilled, meaningless to-do lists and appointments no one ever got to. 'They keep their captives alive, either to feed on them or to sell them or to use them against bigger threats, which their harpoons can't handle. It's disgusting from our point of view, but they're also only trying to survive, you know? I'm pretty torn. But *using* our kind to fight the Ferals?' Izanami shakes her head, and the long curls covering her breasts shift to one side, exposing more skin.

'Pietro says he read about this parasite that burrows into a frog and forces it to grow an extra leg. That extra limb makes the frog a disabled, awkward mess; and the whole point is just so a predator would eat the frog, and the parasite, in turn, burrows into that predator instead. The parasite features as the villain of the story here, but it's just trying to survive, isn't it? The things Pietro reads sometimes—ridiculous.'

And I remember Brad telling me how much he too loves to soak up human culture every chance he gets. I guess he has more in common with Pietro than he cares to admit.

'There's this parasite that creates zombified ants. It's the basis for this post-apocalyptic zombie game I used to play,' I try to contribute to the conversation.

Izanami is accompanying us to where General Wu's troops are based because she says she knows the ins and outs around here. We could have flown to save time, but we can't risk getting shot down again with all the human camps in this area.

That, and the fact that she, apparently, has always wanted to join in the fight, but Pietro has held her back. Because life is short. Because it's not worth risking. His being a strong believer in 'health is wealth' and that kind of thing.

'The *Cymothoa exigua*—now *that's* an interesting parasite,' Pietro's suave baritone pipes in from behind us, and Brad's rolling his eyes again beside him. They both went on ahead to do some reconnaissance of the place, and I guess we're good to go. I told them I've been getting this weird prickle in the back of my neck like we're being followed, but if they say it's safe, then it's safe.

'It picks a good fish host and ultimately *replaces* its tongue.' He comes over to where we're crouched and I fight to keep my eyes from wandering off his face. 'Then it gets all the nourishment from whatever the fish consumes. A handy trick, isn't it?'

'Fascinating,' Brad drawls, and I bite back a giggle. 'We should keep moving.'

We start back down the road again—Ming Yu Outpost shouldn't be too far from where we are now. General Wu gave us specific directions, and even though we've just added more to our numbers, there's no telling what we'll encounter along the way.

Brad, in particular, hasn't stopped fidgeting with the braided strings on his wrist since we left Izanami's lair this morning. He's nervous about the possibility of meeting his hero, to say the least, and I don't blame him.

The Lightbringer is the leader of Brad's people, the greatest of them all—or so they say. When the Hostiles invaded Brad's home planet centuries ago, Brad, as the Harbinger, failed in his duty to warn the Citadel of the incoming threat. Brad was tortured and left for dead—a shadow of what he was before—while the Hostiles laid waste to their planet and claimed it as their own.

The Lightbringer brought as many as he could and somehow escaped to Earth, where they began their new lives hiding out among us in plain sight. It was the Lightbringer who discovered they could Bind with dead human hosts to survive. But then, after a few centuries, the Lightbringer disappeared for no apparent reason. Everyone assumed he was dead. As the Harbinger, Brad was the herald on these distant shores, the one burdened with a task that weighed heavily on his shoulders. His failure haunts him to this day—he's never believed himself to be the leader his people want him to be. Seeing the Lightbringer again will put his insecurities at ease—or better yet, as I'm sure he's hoping, relieve him of his duties, and the Lightbringer can take back the reins and lead them to victory again.

Qing Shan whinnies softly behind me and nudges me back to the present. I pat her nose with a smile.

'You're in good company,' Brad breathes low on my other side. I notice that Pietro and Izanami have moved on ahead of us, Pietro, of course, still naked as the day he was born. I don't think I'll ever get used to his flashing us every time he turns around.

'What do you mean?'

Brad nods to Qing Shan clip-clopping close behind me. 'That's three of my brethren you've saved from a horrible fate now, along with Qing Shan pledging her loyalty to you.' He shrugs. 'At this rate, they'll all follow you and push me farther and farther away from your inner circle. And when we find the Lightbringer, I'll be nothing more than, as humans call it, a regular Joe. Do me a favour and stay where I can keep my eye on you, would you?'

I grin and reach for his hand, 'You just can't wait to let go of this responsibility, can you?'

'I don't want it,' Brad squeezes my hand in reply. 'I'm doing this to keep you safe, Ava. To keep this world safe. But, if someone more qualified happens by, they're welcome to assume my mantle.'

'You'll do just fine,' I assure him. 'You've gotten your people this far. If anything, your Lightbringer should be pleased.'

'If I should be so lucky,' he fiddles with the braids on his wrist again. 'Sometimes, I look back and wonder if the moments of my life that people will remember most are the big gestures, or is it the little things that truly matter? Humans die and funerals are held, a life summarized in syllables and song, packed nice and neat with a few tidy lines, a diary, a letter. But what about the memories no one knows about, the moments you won't see on your highlights reel? A hand withdrawing from yours, a torn photograph, the last slice of pizza, a small heartbreak?'

He runs his other hand on his abdomen ever so casually, but I catch it—the scars on his torso, proof of his mortality, the finality of his existence, for the very first time since they came to this planet.

'I don't need this role to be known, Ava. It's not the way I want to be remembered. I want someone to remember me for my tragedies and my splendour, someone who knows me better than I know myself. The way my spirit burned when I lived and the way my heart broke when I finally left. I have you to thank for that, and that is enough.'

He shares a sad smile with me, and I throw him one right back.

'I can't possibly know you that way, Brad, when I don't even know myself.' My Chucks scrape the side of a worn-out pavement, and I look down at myself. 'I left my whole life behind to join you, believing I can protect my friends from all this suffering. But did I do the right thing? Roy is gone now, crushed beneath the walls of Marcello's, trying to save his dad until his very last breath.'

I swallow. 'Cassie is continents away from me, and I don't even know how she's doing, if she's better off or is she suffering just as much as the rest of the world? Connor has been swept away on this mission he doesn't think he's good enough for. I haven't even heard anything from my Aunt Steph.

'I left Cassie. She saw Roy die and then I left. She had already lost her boyfriend—the last thing she needed was to lose her best friend too. But I left anyway because I'm a coward. And I hate my dad but I miss him, and I wonder whether he's still alive. I'm just glad my mother never got to see any of this and Roy and his dad are out there somewhere, enjoying infinite sundaes wherever they may be.'

Brad shakes his head. 'To find acceptance where you belong doesn't mean forgetting where you came from. It's okay to be sad. It's okay to mourn. Even with this immortality, I still learn something new each day. And accepting grief is what makes the next day brighter, because you know in your heart there must be something better than this.'

He turns my palm towards him and rubs his thumb across my skin. 'Countless times, you've felt you were out of your league, that you couldn't see how you could possibly make a difference. But you're here, are you not? Didn't you once tell me that you chose to be here, that you're no Chosen One?'

I smile in spite of myself. 'Why does your memory have to be so damn sharp?'

'Where you're concerned, it's as sharp as it should be.'

'Save the romantic tête-à-tête for later, lovebirds,' Pietro cuts in and Brad rolls his eyes again—I don't think I've ever seen him scoff this much at anyone. 'Ming Yu Outpost awaits.' Pietro makes a small curtsy and extends his arm out in front of me.

Up ahead, the fabled Ming Yu Outpost comes into view. I don't know why I was expecting some sort of a grand archway or impenetrable fortress when I had this image of the outpost in my mind—maybe I was raising the idea of it too high on a pedestal, like it's some sort of promised land, a last bastion of safety calling out to anyone who seeks refuge, a beacon of hope like those safehouses you always hear about in zombie apocalypse games. Maybe it's the fact that Brad initially instructed me to meet him here, which is why I've always pictured it to have a warmer, softer glow around it, handpicked and perfect from a sea of dreary landscapes and abandoned towns.

But Ming Yu Outpost isn't a bastion—it's barely a structure. It's a temporary shelter with makeshift tents to house twenty, maybe thirty people; campfires on the ground that were never lit; a few boxes of otherworldly concoctions that look similar to the wendigos' potions, which I've seen Harley, our deer-skull-headed party healer, brew. An orange-tinted bottle lies broken on the ground, the only proof of life in an otherwise static and colourless shot.

The human camp where we found the Zheng actually looks more formidable than this.

When we enter the campsite, there's some activity within the tents and groups of men emerge with dull faces and greenish-white skin, all of them in fancy imperial garb like they were plucked straight out of old, black-and-white cinema. They sport traditional coat-like robes, and complete the ensemble with top hats plus a piece of paper pinned to their foreheads that look strange and out-of-place in an apocalypse.

They're Jiangshi too, just like General Wu back in Leslie's base.

One of them, likely the one in charge with the way his glorious braid is flowing down from the back of his head, hops over to Brad and shakes his hand.

'*Huan ying*, Harbinger. My name is Cai Yongliang, captain of the 88th division.' He gestures a stiff arm towards his men, then nods to us. 'General Wu sent word you would come.'

'Thank you for meeting us, Captain Yongliang,' Brad grasps the captain's hand with a firm grip, while part of me worries the corpse's arm might just break off in Brad's clasp. Still, no amount of firmness in his handshake can mask the nerves in Brad's voice. 'You've seen the Lightbringer?'

'Glimpses, Harbinger, and rumours. Are you aware of all the hearsays in these parts, sir?'

Brad shakes his head, but Izanami steps up, clearing her throat, 'Are you talking about the disappearances?' She asks him in her stilted Mandarin, which I can barely understand. The captain indulges her attempt to be respectful all the same.

'*Dui*,' Yongliang nods and turns back to Brad and me. 'Unexplained phenomena all around the world, going back decades and even in these modern times. Entire towns missing, cities disappearing overnight without a trace. Residents gone in the blink of an eye, leaving everything in their homes exactly as they were before they vanished.'

'I've heard of them. Some say the government sends armies to clear out residents within minutes to relocate them elsewhere,' I say. 'Aren't there UFO conspiracies and stuff too?'

'We've been trying to get to the bottom of this mystery for the longest time across different locations. Nothing has been conclusive so far, but the extra-terrestrial origins might actually be more applicable in this case. Please, come with me,' Yongliang turns away and hops towards the tents, and I get the urge to ask him why he and his men didn't hop around with their rigor-mortis stiffened arms extended in front of them.

I do have a pretty good guess—Brad often told me that a lot of their race simply went along with the baseless assumptions made by humans just to stay out of trouble or to seem less of a threat. The hilarious notion of the Jiangshi with their arms sticking out in front of them is, in all likelihood, just another example of humans stereotyping the zombies.

As we weave through the groups of Jiangshi nodding and smiling at us, I realize I'll never get used to these friendly mythological creatures living among us, despite all that I've been through with them. I think about Connor and me farming these cartoon Jiangshi dungeon mobs in one of our favourite MMORPGs, and for a second, I wish this were all just a dream.

It's not, though. Life hasn't been kind to those of us who are left, and if I knew that the last time my life felt normal would be the last time, would I have done everything differently? Would I have hugged Aunt Steph more, dragged my feet to Cassie's cheerleader practices whenever she asked me, asked Roy about the ins and outs of his father's ice cream business, paid more attention to the nameless faces in the halls when I went through high school in a blur? Would I have looked for my father, forgiven him for abandoning me, and accepted the fact that he just never loved me when he left? Would I have smiled more, talked more, laughed more?

Would I have lived?

'We're trying to find a pattern of the disappearances across the country on a map, but we haven't noticed anything definitive yet,' Yongliang goes on as we follow him. 'We camped here because we're trying to see if there's a connection, which is how we found it.'

Brad raises his eyebrows, 'It?'

'There hasn't been much Feral activity here since we arrived, and we think we know why.' Yongliang stops hopping, and in front of us stretches out a clearing where there are no houses, no trees, no plant life whatsoever. There's a single protrusion in the middle of it all, a rocky outcrop that juts out from the ground with a gaping hole for a mouth, like some monstrous subterranean creature bursting out from the depths and meeting its tragic fate up here on the surface, forever frozen in a perpetual moment of rage.

Pietro frowns. 'A cave? That leads to . . . where, exactly?'

'We don't know, and I'm ashamed to say we haven't been brave enough to try again. We have made many attempts, but no one who dared to venture inside ever came back,' Yongliang hangs his head. 'Even now, just as the first tendrils of daylight start to appear, we can hear a rumbling from deep inside, low and ominous. Like something is still hungry. Like it wants . . . more.'

At this, Qing Shan clip-clops to the middle of the clearing, her dragon-tail steady and head held high like she's never been surer of anything in her life. Yongliang hesitates, but I follow and fall in step beside Qing Shan. Brad and the rest come over to stand by my side in front of the mouth of the cave. Qing Shan paws at the ground.

'It's . . . slippery,' I squint at the muddy earth. The mouth of the cave leads down to the depths of god-knows-what at a steep angle, and it was probably too slippery a slope to offer a proper foothold to anyone who ventured out down there.

Qing Shan screeches something low and soft to Zahir, who turns his creepy man-face to Brad.

'There's something down there,' Brad tells Yongliang. 'Zahir and Qing Shan can sense its presence. And judging by the angle of this fancy gateway, I can venture a good guess that it has been enjoying hearty meals ever since your men came sliding down.'

'I can handle this,' Izanami steps to the front of the group and puffs out her impressive bosom. 'If it's a slippery slope you're worried about, let's fashion a net to catch everyone's fall, yes?'

Brad steps aside to give her space. 'Better than asking nicely, I'd say.'

We all move back as Izanami positions herself at the cave's mouth. Her long, spindly spider-legs latch onto the rim of the cave's entrance, and before I can even digest what she's planning to do, she works her magic and spins her web right into the hole and into the darkness below.

'See? Easy-peasy,' she flips her hair over her shoulders and gives us all an eyeful of her generous endowments. 'I don't see why we should—'

The ground beneath our feet shudders. There's a thud like something just bumped its head directly beneath our feet. There's not enough time to register what just happened when Pietro screams Izanami's name. Something shoots out from the cave's dark mouth.

Izanami's confident smile slips. She turns back to the cave just as Pietro lunges for her but he's too late, too late.

Something huge, fast and livid bursts out of the cave. It's an actual mouth, an actual creature, and it rams Izanami squarely in her abdomen and tosses her into the air. Pietro leaps to catch her. Brad shoves me behind him. Yongliang and his men form a circle around us and then it's here, it's out in the open, and it's a dragon.

Eyes white-hot and bloodless, the colossus slithers around the clearing, slow, calculating, its hard scales scraping against the rocks, its head held high above the ground. Years of waiting, stationary and alone inside that cave must've muddied its glorious armour. Beneath the muck and grime and shame flickers the glint of gold here and there, a rainbow-hued shimmer of the creature's elegance from long ago. Now, all that's left is pure, undiluted rage and a profound sorrow, something it must have known too well from decades, even centuries, of motionless solitude, its cavernous mouth forever open and positioned under the cave's opening, waiting for anything and everything that slid straight down into its belly.

But there's something about its loneliness now, something about the way it glares at all of us circling it like we're in a delicate dance. There's something about its plea, like it wants to be freed from this meaningless cycle, a longing for the old life it had before it was cursed with this cave-dwelling existence.

It's another one of Brad's people, another one of the Pure that Binded with a host and lost itself over time.

But it's leering at us now, seething at the way Izanami's web choked its enormous maw, its breathing so powerful that wisps of smoke shoot in and out of its nostrils. I'm hoping against hope that it doesn't actually breathe fire.

It doesn't. Because one of the Jiangshi makes a move—too sudden, too late.

The leviathan attacks.

The Jiangshi spring into action and bombard the dragon with swift kicks to its torso, their stiff hopping a thing of the past. Yongliang barks out commands and both Qing Shan and Zahir join the fray, weaving in and out of harm's way as the behemoth whips its spiked tail around to protect its rear. It picks out Yongliang's men one at a time and Brad throws me a look and surges right into battle himself.

I look around for Izanami.

I spot her crumpled form a little way to my right. Pietro is holding her in his arms as the carnage carries on, but they need him out there more than they do me. This is no time for one of the strongest fighters in the group to hang back and play bench.

'I'll take care of her,' I gasp out to Pietro as I skid to a stop in front of him. 'Please, Pietro, help Brad.'

Pietro clenches his teeth, and his red, otherworldly, all-too-Bradlike eyes narrow at me. 'Thank you,' he whispers, and in an instant, he's gone.

I swallow the lump in my throat and avert my eyes from the dark mess on Izanami's abdomen. I try to conjure up that image of her behind the candy stall from a happier time, her with her thumbs-up sign and her smile intact, but it's no use. Now, her long, furry legs are splayed erratically in all directions on the ground, but to my surprise, it doesn't trigger any sort of fear in me, even though I had told Brad about my aversion to spiders back at Carl and Edna's too long ago. The thought that Izanami was possibly dying in my arms is enough to push all thoughts of silly phobias out of my mind, because who has time for fear during the apocalypse? Who has time for weakness when your friends' lives are at stake?

I try my best to hold Izanami's body in my arms, sending her my warmth, my energy and whatever positive vibes I can summon to keep her holding on. Like I can heal her somehow. Like there's anything else I can do now but watch.

I look up at the chaos unfolding before me as everyone tries to pacify the beast—even Brad is trying to screech to it in between perfectly timed dodges—but it's no use. With this much bottled-up rage clouding the dragon's judgement, I don't think it's in any mood to listen to anything or anyone at all.

But just when the helplessness starts to paralyse me again, something else catches my eye, something moving—or that moved—at the mouth of the cave. I squint at the entrance and there it is—strands of long, fiery red hair that seem to shift in the shadows in an imaginary gust of wind, a pair of eyes watching and waiting, then it blinks and disappears.

Against my better judgement, I squeeze Izanami's hand as she stirs, before laying her gently on the ground. And then, sending up a quick prayer that she'll be all right despite the terrible injury to her stomach, I sprint across to the mouth of the cave while everyone else is preoccupied with the fight.

Someone was here. There are marks on the side of the cave entrance now, marks that weren't there before. Like someone grabbed onto the walls for support to watch the commotion. Someone curious. Someone *inside*.

Careful not to slip on the boggy ground, I step as close to the rim of the cave as I possibly can. And scream.

'Help us, please!' I yell as loud as I can into the abyss. 'We don't want to hurt your dragon—we don't want to hurt anyone! Please! Please help us!'

'Ava!' My plea had caught Brad's attention and I turn around—unfortunately, Brad isn't the only one.

The dragon whips its head around and charges straight at me. 'AVA!'

The raw fear in Brad's voice pierces and breaks my heart because he's scared and I'm scared and I'm going to die now and this is real and the dragon has opened its mouth and all I can see are fangs and blood and me, about to be skewered on one of those massive teeth forever.

But at the last second, it happens.

From behind me, deep within the cave, a screech resounds through the cavern, issuing a powerful command and making us all stop as if we were on pause.

The dragon stops inches from my face, and slowly, slowly, it raises its head before curling its body on the ground like a domesticated snake.

The dust settles. The Jiangshi screech to a halt. Brad is looking at me now, relief and fear and anticipation pooling along the edges of his blood-red eyes. He knows exactly what happened, and I think I do too.

The Lightbringer is alive, and he just spoke to us all.

12

Nerfed

'Afraid.'

I turn to Brad beside me as he takes a deep breath and swallows, my eyes zeroing in on his Adam's apple bobbing in his throat. 'Um. What?'

'I'm afraid. You're wondering how I feel, aren't you?' he whispers, raising the oil lamp Yongliang lent us for my benefit. Brad is gifted with night vision thanks to his alien eyes, but little human me isn't quite so lucky. 'You've been tiptoeing around me since we got here.'

'I—' Why am I always so transparent to this man? 'This is the moment of truth for you. I just want you to know I'm here.'

'I know. I know you are. Thank you.' He sighs. 'Thank you.'

We trek deeper into the cave. When the dragon's rampage died down a while ago, Brad was able to ask it to help lower us down into the Lightbringer's cove, just the two of us. I know he needs me here for moral support, but I'm not sure just how much of a help I can be to him when he's clearly a bundle of nerves.

I can understand the sentiment—he's been waiting for this moment for centuries, after all. I know the Lightbringer is their leader and all, but I honestly can't wrap my head around the idea that anyone would just leave his people like that and disappear without a word. It just feels irresponsible to go into hiding just because he couldn't be bothered anymore.

Naturally, for Brad's sake, I won't wear my prejudices on my sleeve. If meeting his hero is going to give him that little push he needs to lead his people to victory, then I'm all for it.

Just when I start to wonder how deep this cave actually goes, Brad suddenly grips my hand and we both stop. I look up from the ground.

Seated atop a pile of flat rocks is a man dressed in rags, hunched over his own form like he's trying to meditate but failing miserably. Long, dishevelled red hair springs from the top of his head and cascades all over him and down to the ground like a bloody waterfall, a chaos of a mess covering a chaos of a face. He looks old—older than gods, older than time—his crumpled skin a mix of green and brown and white and red, like someone had played a prank on him and had spray-painted his entire body with a gradient display of the four primary colours in stark contrast to the dullness of his face.

Brad sucks in his breath beside me, then takes a second to recover. 'Lightbringer,' he whispers, then clears his throat, 'Lightbringer.'

He repeats the second word with a firmer, stronger tone, and the man before us stirs. As he moves, the colours on his skin shift with him, blending and changing and reminding me that we have a shape-shifter in our midst as Jimmy once told me, the only one of their race who can change his appearance at will.

The Lightbringer then raises his head and makes eye contact, and it's only then I see the livid scar across his throat, like someone, or something, had tried to chop his head off and . . . failed. What's even more disturbing is the obsidian black of his eyes. That's all there is to them—black orbs with no irises or pupils in sight.

And, as the final nail on the coffin of my disappointment at this pathetic mess in front of me, he croaks out.

'You shouldn't have come.'

* * *

The Lightbringer's face is cracked and chapped like it had eroded over time and had been haphazardly reassembled. His dark, dark eyes reflect no emotion at all—no sadness, no remorse, nothing. They're just pits, full and empty all at once. But his voice conveys all the loneliness he has borne over the centuries. It's the feeling of a soundless sheet of rain enveloping the world, more than a light drizzle but not quite a downpour.

A lingering uneasiness.

But despite the melancholy in his voice, the cracks in his face look maddened—chafed, antagonized, and it reminds me too much of a Hostile, beneath the armour a twisted face with an exoskeleton.

'You should leave.'

'Lightbringer—'

'Leave.' The Lightbringer cuts Brad off. 'There is nothing more to say here.'

'Please.' Brad takes a step forward, his fists balled. 'It won't be long now before the first wave is over. We need you. We need our leader.'

'They've got you, haven't they?' The cracks in the Lightbringer's face seem to seethe. 'The Harbinger is all your people need.'

'*Our* people.' Brad heaves a sharp gasp, a flicker of hurt crossing his face. 'I am no one.'

'You are all they have,' the Lightbringer rasps. 'You've had your chance. If you've learned nothing since we arrived here, Harbinger, then you're not fit to lead. Your inadequacy is not my problem.'

I watch as the words sear through Brad's face, breaking any last shred of his feigned bravery. His desperation strains across the infinite space between his leader and himself, but it's a gap he can't breach, and for the first time, Brad is at a complete loss.

I clench my fists. 'You're a jerk, you know that?'

At this, the Lightbringer's black gaze bores into me. 'What?'

'You heard me,' I stomp over to his pretentious pile of rocks and grit my teeth. 'I've been hearing all these wonderful things about you from Luna and Ethan and Jimmy, that you're supposed to be this all-powerful and respectable leader who wouldn't be caught dead hiding out like a coward in his stupid hole, cowering behind his dragon, doing this stupid meditation shit like you're enlightened or something. It's just a load of bull and you're an ass. You abandoned your people—*your* people—when they needed you the most, and now when they need you again, you're sitting here, waiting out the end of the world because you're a pathetic mess.'

I point a trembling finger at his cracked face, 'That makes you a Class-A jerk, and frankly, you make me sick. So if you're not going to take responsibility for the people *you brought here in the first place*, you're better off dead.'

I turn on my heel and catch a glimpse of Brad's horrified expression. I grab his hand and yank him along, 'Let's go. We're wasting our time with this worm.'

'Ava, isn't it?' the Lightbringer whispers, and I clench my jaw. 'I heard the Harbinger calling out to you outside.'

I don't turn around.

'Do you even know what you're saying, or what you're heading into?' he goes on, his voice growing more feeble with every word. 'I doubt that you do, or you wouldn't have joined this little crusade in the first place.'

He's baiting me. 'I don't think you've earned the right to condescend to me,' I turn back. 'You have no idea what I've been through.'

'And yet you didn't hesitate to do the same to me, did you?' the Lightbringer throws me an amused smile, but it only makes his cracked face even more grotesque. 'You said all these things without even knowing who I am. That's the same kind of snap judgement you're fighting against. You don't know what I've been through, do you? There's an easy remedy for that, of course.' The Lightbringer steps down from his throne of rubble and hobbles over to Brad and me.

'Indulge me, Ava, and let me tell you a story.'

* * *

Heavy.

An unbearable weight presses down on him, a force so massive it suffocates him from the inside. The world is collapsing around him, but it's not—he's alive, he's safe. There are no explosions, no faraway tremors, no lullaby of screams and final death rattles. He's somewhere else now, his planet gone, his people lost.

He's lost. He doesn't know how long he's been here or how they managed to survive the crash. How they destroyed all evidence of their ship, how his people scattered to every corner of this . . . this place. All he knows is what he taught them, what they needed to do to survive.

The Binding is what they called it. Like it was sacred. Like it was noble. Like it was something that would make them feel whole.

But it wouldn't, would it? They'll always be incomplete. They'll always be refugees, always unwelcome, always straddling what's real and what's not. That's something he can never give his people, can never even hope to help them with. While he's given them a means to survive, he hasn't given them the one thing they need to live truly meaningful lives.

He hasn't given them peace.

They're still here, still wavering, still wandering, still maimed by the memories of their home, still haunted by the Hostiles that will always have a hold on them.

At this, he finally opens his eyes.

The weight pressing down on him, he discovers, is on the inside; it's his own heart telling him he doesn't deserve to live, doesn't deserve to be here. He was the first. The one who discovered this so-called ability, this traitorous Binding. A shape-shifter is what they called him, like it was a blessing, not a curse. Like it was something he could wield, not something he had to live with.

He looks down at his hands. Today, he is a monster. Tomorrow, he can be a man.

His hands, they're scarred—invisible wounds that betray the evils he has done, the havoc he has wrought. He touches a tentative finger to his face, and they're still there. The cracks. Almost like he had desperately tried to shed his skin but failed. Because he knows what he is, and he can't hide it; he can't outrun himself.

The Lightbringer is a joke, he thinks. He doesn't deserve the loyalty, the gratitude. He doesn't deserve this life.

Because when he piloted the ship to where they crashed, it wasn't his ship. It was something he had commandeered . . . and he hadn't been alone in the cockpit.

He had to . . . get rid of the original owner. He had to. And when he crashed, he Binded. For the very first time. To survive.

He Binded with the Hostile.

And here he is. A shape-shifter, a leader, a lie.

The Lightbringer is a lie.

* * *

Brad takes a step back as soon as the Lightbringer finishes his story, like his words had the power to shove him with physical force. The revelation mars me, just as the Lightbringer raises a withered hand to his face in shame.

The Lightbringer brought the Pure here to Earth and taught them to survive in Earth's atmosphere by Binding with human hosts, and the only way that he could've possibly known that was because he had tried it first himself. Only there weren't any human corpses around where they first crashed, were there? It was just the Hostile pilot whom he had overpowered to steal the ship, and the atmosphere of a foreign planet that was killing him one breath at a time.

Desperation. It pushes us all over the edge. And for the Lightbringer, he did what he had to do. Suddenly, the cracked face makes much more sense.

'I am losing my mind, dear Ava, one day at a time. And I've had many days.' There's a break in his voice now that wasn't there before. 'Too many years, too many physical forms, too many attempts to escape. But it's still me, trapped inside this . . . shell, still the same guilt and fear gnawing at me from within.

'My last attempt to escape was to let someone behead me, but even that was something I wasn't noble enough to carry through,' he tilts his head to caress the horizontal scar across his neck. 'At the last minute, my body changed, and the monster inside stopped the blade from making the cut.'

He smiles at me now, again and in pain, an expression that pulls the cracks on his face taut. 'I want none of this endless cycle. I shouldn't have brought the Pure here. We should have all died along with our planet. And if the Hostiles come and take over, then maybe they should—maybe they deserve it. Maybe it's the natural order of things, something that I in my conceit shouldn't have meddled with.'

He turns away and hobbles back to his rocky throne, snatching away all hopes of redemption with him.

Disappointment is a many-faceted thing, a persistent disquiet, a chagrin that refuses to let go. With the way the Lightbringer punctuated his tale, I'm ready to accept defeat.

But not Brad.

He springs from beside me and he's right in front of the Lightbringer with his fist clenched and his face contorted. It takes a second for me to see the hurt in his red eyes as he grits his teeth.

And clobbers the Lightbringer right across his cracked face.

The Lightbringer stumbles. Brad follows it up with another slug, and another, and another, until the Lightbringer crashes onto the cold, rocky ground and Brad bounds on top of him to continue his onslaught. The pummelling doesn't let up. Brad screeches at his leader, fevered tears pooling in his ruby eyes.

Then.

The Lightbringer screeches back.

In one swift motion, he shoves Brad away and the next thing I see is Brad slamming against the opposite wall of the cave, the Lightbringer's grip wound tight around his neck.

'You . . . *dare?*' The Lightbringer hisses, and his spindly fingers lift Brad against the wall. Brad claws at his throat, his feet dangling in the air, his face a mix of pain and betrayal.

'Stop, please!'

'This has nothing to do with you, human.'

'Please! You're killing him,' I plead. 'Please stop . . .'

The Lightbringer narrows his ebony eyes at me and then at Brad, whose struggles grow weaker and weaker. A single tear has trickled down the side of the Lightbringer's cheek, and I realize that I'm crying too, crying for him.

At this, the Lightbringer loosens his grip. Brad crumples to the ground and I rush to wrap my arms around him.

'Leave. Please,' the Lightbringer whispers to me, and I glance up at the tears that have caked in the cracks.

'We are trapped in the madness of life and lies, Ava, and I will have none of it.'

* * *

The trudge back to the mouth of the cave is agony. Brad doesn't say a word to me, but he doesn't have to—I can feel his aggression and shame mixed together and crushed and packed and overflowing and snowballing into something he doesn't know how to deal with. And it's tangible, this ball, this weight. It bears down on him with his every step, and if I could help him carry the load, I would.

But he won't let me. Every so often, he rubs the hateful marks the Lightbringer's fingers left on his neck, like he had been branded and would carry that mark with him from here on out. Brad once told me that we all share the same heart now, and that it's just as maddening for him when this heart that doesn't even belong to him writhes and thrives and breaks. It's calling out to me now, his heart. It's clawing against his chest, pleading, afraid. Anywhere but here. Anything to escape this pain.

Which is why when we resurface and are met with Yongliang's harried eyes, it takes a while for me to register what he's saying.

The Avem. General Wu. Something about an attack, urgent, something. I have to blink to clear the fog from my mind.

'Connor,' Yongliang says, and it's the first word that gets through to me with any clarity.

'Connor?'

'The Avem has sent word from General Wu,' Yongliang repeats for my benefit. 'Qing Feng Outpost is preparing for an incoming attack.'

My heart drops. 'Ferals?'

And the Captain's next words knock out whatever energy's left in me. 'Handlers. Two of them.'

I turn to Brad beside me, but he's still lost, still with nowhere else he wants to go.

I grind my teeth. 'We need to move.'

Brad looks at me then for the first time since the madness in the cave. And his eyes herald the words that I know will betray me.

'I can't.'

'Brad?'

'I can't,' he whispers. 'I . . . I have to stay here. I have to bring the Lightbringer back into the fold.'

'Brad, listen to me.' I grab his shoulders. What was once so firm and indomitable now feels vanquished, done.

'He's not coming. We don't need him, and right now, our friends do. We need to go to Qing Feng Outpost.'

Brad searches my eyes for pity, understanding, anything— whatever it would take to convince me to stay, to tell him he's right, to let him fight this impossible fight of forcing his leader to change his mind. But I've let Cassie slip away from me before— I'm not letting Connor do the same. So I'm pleading with Brad's eyes just as fiercely, just as desperately. I need him to be rational. I need him to be strong. I need him to be the brave Harbinger everyone wants him to be. I need him to be Brad.

My Brad.

But he's lost in there somewhere, still trapped beneath all the vulnerabilities, still raw like a gaping wound, still that same Watcher on Distant Shore with his own redemption forever out of reach.

My eyes well up, and so do his. The unspoken argument breaks my heart then, because I know that he's already made his choice, and he knows I've made mine.

'Ava . . . '

'I have to go.' I fight to keep my voice steady. There is everything and nothing in the space between us now, and I clench my fists to feign bravery. I've been feigning a lot of things over these past few days, borrowing emotions and traits that aren't mine, like I'm overcompensating for all the helplessness around me by taking on that bravado for everyone else.

But there's disappointment and loneliness in here now, and did I borrow that too? Like the forgotten photographs in the office cubicles and the shadows on the hangers, did I take on what was theirs, or is this feeling mine alone?

'Tell your men to pack up,' I say to the captain this time, who nods. 'We're not wasting any more time here.'

I start marching away from the cave with twice the effort, like my own body doesn't want to, like every part of me wants to turn back to where Brad is standing, watching me leave without even bothering to ask me to stay. But turning back now will only give those eyes a hold on me, and I don't trust myself to turn away twice.

I walk past Pietro who's carrying a now-stable Izanami in his arms. His ruby eyes flicker between me and Brad in an unspoken question. When I don't speak, he readjusts the position of his sleeping wife in his arms, clears his throat, and follows me.

When I climb onto Qing Shan's back, Zahir throws me a sad smile with his creepy man-face before he pads back to Brad. Yongliang hops over to screech the coordinates to Qing Feng Outpost to Qing Shan, then he nods up at me, his army of Jiangshi behind him armed and ready. He looks at me with something like sympathy in his eyes too, and I realize that I'm crying. When did that happen?

Taking a deep breath, I stroke the shimmering dragon scales over Qing Shan's neck and she rears up, screeching a final screech, before breaking into a gallop at top speed, our little party of creatures following right behind me, away from the cave, away from the Lightbringer.

Away from Brad.

13

X Joins Your Party

On the day we had a particularly long match of *Nebula Battles*, I brushed past the school gates to find Connor leaning against a tree by the sidewalk. He was wearing one of those turtleneck sweaters and navy blazers he loves so much, and next to him, pale little me in my school uniform didn't shine as bright.

But seeing him there with the glasses on his nose and the high ponytail on his head and his arms folded oh-so-casually across his chest, Connor being Connor and just there *waiting* for me, made my heart skip a beat.

'Hey.'

'Hey yourself,' I greeted back, vaguely aware of the pairs of female eyes glued to him right now as I walked over. 'Cassie will be late. She's got cheerleader practice today.'

'I know. I'm not here for Cassie.'

'You're here for me?'

He shrugged.

'Okay. What's up?'

'Nothing much. You up for a game today?'

I raised an eyebrow at him, trying so damn hard to shove my giddiness as far back down my throat as possible. 'You waited for me after school just to see if I'm free to play *Nebula Battles* with you?'

'Yeah. Why? Is that weird?'

'No,' I bit my lip. 'I'm always up for a game.'

'Great,' he pushed himself off the tree trunk and shoved a hand into his pocket, the height of college cool for high-school me. 'Let's go.'

It wasn't like there was a designated spot where we could play *Nebula Battles* to our heart's content—Canyon Falls wasn't that fancy. To play the real-time strategy game we both loved so much, we both had to be in our own homes, in our own chairs, in front of our own computers, swearing and screaming over the headphones.

So really, Connor waiting for me after school was wholly unnecessary. He would have to walk me home, then walk to his own home before we could even start playing together.

But, strolling beside him down the streets at a slow and deliberate pace like that . . . I wasn't about to complain.

'Are you excited about your graduation?' he had both his hands in his pockets now, throwing a totally aloof sideways glance at me.

'Not really. I'm not even sure what I want to do after all this.'

He frowned, 'Aren't you heading into the city with Cassie?'

'No . . . I don't know,' I sighed. 'This Ivy League dream she has? It just doesn't feel like it's right for me.'

'Maybe it isn't,' Connor's lips tugged to the right in a wry smile. 'Maybe you're meant for bigger things.'

'What's bigger than going to college in the most prestigious universities?' I grinned. 'Isn't that what you're doing after you graduate? Go big and all-out with the Brady empire?'

The smile faded. 'I got a job in game dev.'

'That's awesome!'

'In London.'

'Oh.'

'Yeah.'

We strolled along in silence for a while, me being awkward and never knowing what to say. He didn't tell me what he wanted that day—I guess he never did know how. All the skirting around seems so pointless now, but back then there was nothing else to do, and nothing more to say.

'Ava . . .'

'Yeah?'

He stopped and I stopped along with him, gazing up expectantly into those steely eyes behind his glasses. I imagined him asking me to come with and we could leave everything behind and live like we were proper fools, and maybe we were. I thought about lying underneath a sky dotted with stars that watched us and waited for us, and I'd be in his arms with my sighs and my giggles and I'd ask him about our future. You, he'd tell me, you're my future. And I'd smile and it'd be cheesy but we won't care, won't care, won't care.

But all he did that day was look at me like the very image of me was poison, and all I did was stare back at him and it's the kind of madness that should've brought us together but it didn't.

It didn't, because I'm still here, and Connor is elsewhere, and the madness of this world has caught up with us.

My heart pulses in my throat now, back in the chasm of the present. There are no *Nebula Battles* tournaments, no after-school rendezvous, no unspoken feelings to tiptoe around. All there is now are the Ferals and the two Handlers, who are about to ravage the outpost where Connor was supposed to be safe.

Looking back, I guess it was kind of a date even though it wasn't. How simple it all was back then, when we were young and stupid and easily swayed by that meaningless little dance. The unfinished sundaes and the late-night chats. The times when the servers were down and all we had were the ones and zeroes between us. The three-star campaigns and the magic of his laughter. The tragedy of the words that died in our throats and the ghost of the hand I never got to hold.

I'm coming, Connor, and I'm sorry. I wrap my arms more tightly around Qing Shan's neck and shut my eyes.

I'm sorry.

* * *

'I'm sorry.'

A disembodied voice floats through the haze in my mind; but where am I? Wasn't I just charging through the abandoned cities and the broken streets on Qing Shan, a small army of mythological creatures by my side?

'Can you hear me?'

Why can't I see anything, feel anything?

'If you can, I said I'm sorry.'

Am I dreaming, or am I awake?

'I'm sorry it had to be this way, but your friends wouldn't cooperate.'

My friends?

'I thought *you* would, but then you whipped out that pesky little knife of yours and lopped off my guard's pinkie. Now he won't be able to lock up those cages for a week.'

What?

'This is tiresome.' Whoever is speaking sighs and pauses for a beat.

And slaps me hard right across my cheek.

I flinch the moment I taste the blood in my mouth, but has that always been there? Part by part, my body comes alive, slowly, maddeningly, second by second as if powering up a run-down machine. The first thing I feel is the blinding headache, then every muscle follows suit like my body is suddenly remembering the beating it just went through, my insides bruised and clawing for release. I try to wriggle free of whatever I'm in, but haphazard cords cut into my wrists and I realize that my hands are bound behind my back.

I open my eyes.

I'm in a tent. Just like the one where I found the Zheng. It's dark and stuffy and grimy, and here, right in front of me, is a scrawny little man I swear I remember from somewhere.

'Ah, good. You're up. Now we can have a proper conversation.' He pulls up a rickety chair. Seated across from him in close proximity like this, I realize where I've seen him before.

It's Sneery Glasses Guy.

'I'm guessing you're in agony, with all the blood on you and all. But it's a necessary precaution—I want you in your most receptive mental state for all the questions I have for you.' He flashes me that trademark sneer, then clears his throat. 'So, tell me how I can break your friends.'

I lift my head and wince as every joint in my body wails in protest at the small movement.

'You know: personal quirks, odd little hobbies, things that are emotional triggers. Basically weaknesses, what they care about, whom they're with,' Sneery Glasses Guy shrugs. 'Loved ones are always a plus—threatening their safety gets 'em every time.'

I try to lift my head again, but a pained wheeze escapes my lips and it's only then that I register the gash across my cheek—a wound he must've reopened when he slapped me a while ago. Now the taste of rust in my mouth makes more sense.

'Geez. Did my men rough up your brain so bad you can't speak?' he scowls. 'You've still got your tongue, haven't you?'

My mind races through every single thing I've filed in there, straining to recall what the heck happened. How did it all come to this?

'The sooner you tell me about your friends' emotional baggage, the sooner I can break them and the sooner we can all call it a day, go home and have a nice bowl of rice porridge.'

Qing Shan and I were riding through another abandoned town with no plans of stopping. But what was the last one we crossed?

'Proper meals like that are hard to come by these days, but I can get you one if you'd just cooperate.'

I remember hurtling past one of those commercial, fast-food, dim-sum chains I had always planned to try if I ever visited the country as a tourist. Aunt Steph was always bragging about it, telling me authenticity is subjective and that I should try the mass-produced dumplings before I make any snap judgments.

'Don't knock it' til you've tried it, right?' she had winked at me. 'Isn't that what they say?'

I was halfway through daydreaming about what a tour with Aunt Steph would be like, how we would stop by the night markets and she would force stuff I didn't want on me, how she would flit from place to place to make the most of our itinerary and fuss about cramming as many tourist-trap activities as possible into our day, down to the very last second. Then, on the last day, she'd raid the airport shop for souvenirs and ruin our perfectly packed luggage, then stuff them all in an extra carry-on with all the freebies from the flight home and she'd grin at me and I'd grin at her and we'd be tired, our pockets would be empty, and our hearts would be full.

But just when I was trying to shake off the dangerous nostalgia from my mind, something happened. Something big. Something sudden. Something so numerous we couldn't brace for impact.

'You'd like that, wouldn't you?' Sneery Glasses Guy is still not done. 'A nice, steaming-hot bowl of rice porridge?'

Like a deluge, agile beasts poured out from behind houses and atop buildings, a flood of fangs and claws and tails and horns, leaping out from the shadows and holding us where we were. They were everything the loud and clumsy Ferals were not—fast, silent, unified.

As the fog in my mind clears, the image of a horde of leopard-esque creatures sears itself back into my memory—lonely eyes and horned heads and five tails behind each back.

A huge pack of Zheng.

They attacked us.

The shock of the memory elicits a visceral response and I cough at the betrayal. Specks of blood splatter across my jeans and over my bound feet.

'Watch it!' Sneery Glasses Guy nudges his chair away from me. 'God. Still nothing?'

My chest constricts. Something hot threatens to scald my eyelids.

What have I gotten us into now?

'Fine,' he motions for something—to someone, I'm not sure anymore—and a burly man stomps over. 'Perhaps you'll be more talkative when we've loosened your jaw. Be back in a bit.'

He scrapes his chair back, but I never do discover where he heads off to. A sudden force yanks my hair back and I catch a glimpse of the man in front of me, clenching his fist right before he lands the punch, square in my stomach.

The force of the blow knocks the wind out of me, literally. A cry of anguish rips throughout the tent; it's mine and I'm falling; I taste the tang of coins in my mouth before I crash sideways onto the ground, along with the chair.

And it all fades away.

* * *

'I'm no stranger to the emptiness, to the sense of abandonment. Our kind can't have children,' Brad told me once, when we were alone under a blanket of stars, our hearts fighting for a chance to be together when the world was a mess. 'But my men—they're all family. Each and every one of them,' he said. 'So, if you're looking for family, Ava, you have it. Here. With me.'

The first fingers of daylight filter through the gap in the tent and I squint. I don't know how long I've been here, but somebody must've picked me up from the ground because I'm sitting upright on the rickety chair again, all tied up nicely for the next round of abuse. Wherever these men are holding my friends captive can't be very far, and I certainly don't think they're faring any better than I am.

In fact, I can safely say that whatever they're going through is much, much worse. They can handle it better than I can, of course, and my friends are no cowards—but every so often, amid the din of humans marching back and forth outside wherever the hell this is, it breaks through—a sharp cry, a whimper, a low moan, a plea. The unmistakable hint of desperation amidst the chaos outside—the Jiangshi are being tortured too, Qing Shan and Pietro and Izanami with them.

Izanami. She hasn't even recovered from the dragon's onslaught and now she's going through another round of hell.

The reality of my situation dawns on me more clearly now, and the helplessness starts to seep in. Ever since the invasion began, all I've been trying to do is to steel myself to the point of callousness, but despite everything that's happened, why does it still feel like I'm stuck in a monotone of sorts, marking off each day in the calendar just to make it through unscathed? And maybe I am, or maybe I'm not, or maybe the scathing has always been on the inside, hungering and festering and the beginning of the end.

What was I before all this? The pixelated games and the faceless avatars and the life no one remembers, the life no one will miss. After everything we've been through, why does it still feel like nothing's changed, or maybe I haven't changed? Why does that feel so tragic?

Why does that thought break my heart?

A blast of light bursts through the front flap of the tent and it's Sneery Glasses Guy, this time without the brute beside him.

He pulls up his chair and sits down in front of me again, a full-on scowl carved on his face.

'Here's the thing,' he says. 'I've been contemplating letting the leopards have their fill, but honestly, you're skin and bone, and I don't think devouring you piece by piece is going to be even remotely pleasing or fulfilling for them. So.'

He claps his hands and I flinch by instinct. 'I figured I would just turn up the torture for the flaky-skinned guys until they break. The spidery woman is already broken, and the naked one is easy—he's sticking to the girl like glue. All I need now is info on the dragon-horse thing. You can do that, can't you? That's just one little thing as opposed to dirt on all of them.'

'The leopards . . .' My voice scrapes out of my throat all broken and raspy. 'How . . .?'

'Torture someone long enough, break down their sense of identity and self-worth, and you can compel them to do whatever you want them to. I'm hoping I can do the same to your little band of merry men here; so, if you don't mind . . . I don't have all day.' He shrugs like it's no big deal, and something glints against his chest in that movement.

Sneery Glasses Guy has somehow gotten hold of my dog whistle and is now wearing it around his neck like a trophy. I fume.

'Monster.'

'Me? A monster?' he shakes his head and wags a firm finger in my face. 'A monster wouldn't build survivor camps and take people in and feed them fucking rice porridge because the world has gone to shit. A monster wouldn't find a way—a desperate, difficult, but necessary way—to protect the survivors who come straggling in because humans should all be *on the same side.*'

He pauses on that last note for effect, before going on, 'Those unwanted visitors outside, on the other hand, those gigantic horned freaks with the death they bring and those humanlike inner mouths—have you seen one up close? *Those* things are monsters, and all I did was create my own weapons to defend against them. We need monsters to fight monsters, so tell me—how does that make *me* a monster?'

'Because they're not *weapons*, and they're on our side,' I plead, switching to a different tactic. Could this man, somehow, still have a shred of humanity in him? 'And, if you would just please let us go, we can help you. We can keep you safe from the Ferals.'

'Hah! Good one,' he grins. 'The Ferals, you say? Has a nice ring to it. Which just convinces me all the more that you do know so much more about all this than you let on, and I want it. All of it. I want to know everything.'

I grit my teeth, and he sighs. 'Of course, if you still don't feel like talking, I'll just break your friends and be done with it. I'd rather take a shortcut, to be honest, but if you're not going to help, what further use are you? The beasts outside can have their way with you, if that's what you want.'

He scrapes back his chair and panic wails from my chest. There's nobody who can help me now—no Siv or Luna or Connor, no band of hopping corpses or flying mounts. There's no immortal alien boyfriend either, because I've just gone and left him alone to wallow in his self-pity, and I'm pretty sure we just broke up, if we were ever even together.

There's just me now, plain, unremarkable, non-Chosen One me, with nothing else and no one else around.

But I sure as hell am not going to die here.

'Wait! Please,' I croak out just before Sneery Glasses Guy raises the tent's flap. 'Please don't leave me here. I'll . . . I'll tell you everything you need to know.'

'Oh my god—it's about time,' he rolls his eyes, pushes his glasses up his nose and sits back down. 'I'd rather get this over with as soon as possible.'

'I . . .'

'Yes?'

I open my mouth in a whisper. Sneery Glasses Guy leans in.

And I ram my head as hard as I can against his.

He curses and stumbles back and I launch myself towards him as far as my bound limbs will allow. I bite down on my whistle dangling around his neck and tug with all the force I can muster.

We crash down to the ground together and before he can get his bearings, I blow on the whistle as loud as I can. Nothing happens.

'You bitch!' he scrambles up and kicks his booted foot right into my stomach. I grunt, cough out the whistle and lie there gasping, my hands and feet still bound and the chair still intact. 'What the fuck was that for? Your whistle didn't even make a sound!'

He kicks me again out of spite and this time, blood spews out of my mouth. 'Keep your stupid whistle! You can rot here for all I care. I don't even—'

He stops short. A commotion rumbles outside the tent, growing louder and rowdier as the seconds tick by. The shouts of panic turn into howls of terror, and then, we both hear it.

A shrill, high-pitched squeal, the monstrous sound of a monstrous creature—one, no, two of them, running amuck through the camp because I called them, because I confused them, because that silent whistle did exactly what I wanted it to do.

'You—' Sneery Glasses Guy widens his eyes at me, then promptly rushes out of the tent.

The wailing continues. I can only imagine the tortured Zheng fighting the Ferals right now, but I don't want to wait around for the fight to come to me and get trampled underfoot.

I wriggle. This wooden chair won't hold up much longer, which is exactly why launching myself down was part of my haphazard plan. I send out a silent prayer that I can roll myself out of bondage, until the chair's weakened joints squeak.

The legs break off first. I scramble to my feet, operating on pure adrenaline. Then, I lean back and slam backwards against the ground again.

The back of the chair breaks.

I'm free.

I grab a splinter of wood and shiv my way out of the tethers around my wrist, cutting myself in the process. I hold back the tears as soon as I free my hands and feet, shove the pain into the deepest recesses of my mind, and dash out of the tent.

The camp is in shambles. It's a lot bigger than the one we snuck into to look for Pietro, but it's obviously under the same regime, and right now, their leader is nowhere to be seen.

His men, however, are everywhere. They're not mercenaries, not big buff brutes, nothing even remotely like trained fighters who can withstand the onset of an apocalypse. They're just regular people, ordinary men and women who must've been rescued off the streets, stragglers with nowhere else to go and no one to turn to when the end of the world arrived unannounced at their doorstep.

Everywhere I turn, these 'men' are wielding anything that can be picked up and used as a weapon—kitchen knives, screwdrivers, wooden poles, metal rods, baseball bats and even broken glass. There are a few men armed with proper guns and other incendiary firepower, but most of them aren't.

Most of them are just survivors, doing their best to live one more day.

Sneery Glasses Guy had to do what he had to do. And right now, they're facing two wild Ferals using an army of Zheng who had to be tortured to comply.

With this dark realization hanging over my head, I turn to my right and another commotion erupts. We're not alone in this war, and we all have our reasons for doing what we do. We can't save everyone, so we save those we can—some fight for vengeance, some for survival, and most because there's nothing else left to do.

Some, though, fight because they love, and love can prove to be the most dangerous double-edged sword anyone can wield in battle.

Pietro is wielding that weapon right now with reckless abandon, making short work of monsters and men alike, on full berserker mode and wearing the weighted mantle of his heartbreak around him. This creature, this being—this 'brother' of Brad—bounds and rips his way through the camp, and my chest crumples with each mighty hack he makes. Watching him now, it's not the speed or the power or my fear that roots me to the spot—it's his sorrow, his pain, screaming for sympathy now from anything, anyone, and if I looked hard enough, I can almost see the specks fleeing from the corners of his steely eyes with each blow.

At the end of the day, no amount of power or invulnerability can shield the heart when it breaks.

I sprint into the nearest tent. It's empty, save for a few medical supplies and bowls of half-eaten food abandoned in a hurry. Clothes lie scattered everywhere on the ground too, like whoever lived here packed their bags in a hurry because there was no time, no time, no time.

I grab two small knives from the table. I try not to dwell on the fact that there are children-sized clothes in there too, as I rush out.

Pietro is done. The last thing I see before the silence descends is him leaping to grab the Feral by the horns and slamming its head down on the ground with such force that it stays down. It's now lying next to the other Feral at Pietro's feet, both bathed in a pool of their own filth. Radiating around him like an unholy circle are a few tortured Zheng, unconscious but alive, and even further out are the 'warriors' of this camp, shuffling and hobbling, undone and petrified. Brad had never wanted any of them to kill humans, so I can only imagine Pietro's restraint.

At the centre of this ring of despair is the immortal himself, agonizing and shaking and staring down at his own bloodied hands. He trembles into one of the tents to his left and I hurry after him.

He's kneeling on the ground now, and for the first time without all the destruction around him, I see how his once-perfect body is now scarred in all places, angry, open wounds oozing blood from his skin, dark bruises mushrooming all over his chest. He's holding an unconscious Izanami against his body, and the torture has marred her too. One of her eight legs is bent at an unnatural angle and lies limp and withered.

'Pietro . . .'

He looks up at me and the red eyes widen, and I realize I must look terrible too, bloodied and battered just as badly.

'Ava, I . . .' he grits his teeth. 'They ambushed us. Held a knife at Izanami's throat. I . . . couldn't even put up a fight. If the Ferals hadn't come and given me my opening, I . . .' A tear trickles down his cheek, and he doesn't bother to wipe it away. 'I'm sorry.'

I shake my head. 'No, *I'm* sorry, Pietro. I led us here.' I kneel in front of Izanami and hover a hand over her chest. 'Is she . . .?'

'Barely,' Pietro chokes out. 'I . . . need to take care of her, Ava. I can't lose—'

'I know,' I hold Pietro's hand and give it a reassuring squeeze. 'I know. Thank you. For everything.'

He squeezes my hand back and with one last look at Izanami, I force myself to turn away and head back out into the madness.

I'm about to dash into the next tent to look for the Jiangshi when I notice Sneery Glasses Guy in my peripheral vision, sneaking out of the camp like he's heading somewhere more important than this. The image of Izanami and Pietro in the tent, husband and wife tortured until their hearts and spirits shattered, consumes me.

I grip my knives and sprint towards this camp's so-called leader, a mania of wrath.

I turn the corner of a looted sneaker shop, closing the gap between us. I catch up with him just as my own injuries catch up with me, and I reach out to grab his shirt. We both stumble to the ground. I squeeze every last ounce of adrenaline left in me to bear my knee down on his chest and keep his struggling to a minimum. He yelps.

'You!' I hiss, holding the knife to his throat.

'Don't kill me!' The snivelling coward holds up his hand to his face. 'Please! I was only trying to do what was best for us! For humanity!'

I growl at him and push my knee harder against his chest, and he wheezes.

'Please,' he coughs. 'Please—'

The hand holding my blade starts to tremble, and at this moment, his eyes shift from my face to some point behind my ear. He smiles.

'Ah,' he sneers, his snivelling forgotten. 'My hard work is finally paying off.'

Against my better judgement, I turn to see whatever it is he's smiling at, and my heart drops.

Padding through the grass and mud are packs of Zheng, their heads bowed, their eyes trained on me, their shoulders hunched and ready to pounce. Their tails swish gracefully in the wind as they surround me, and if I weren't about to be mauled by those single horns on their foreheads, they would've actually looked magnificent.

Sneery Glasses Guy chortles, 'I would strongly suggest you let me go now, if you don't want to be ripped apart by these creatures you love so much.'

I get up and brace myself, gripping my measly knives as hard as I can. My wounds have gotten the better of me now and it's so, so tempting to just lie down and give up. I could close my eyes and go to sleep, and I'll never see Connor or Cassie or Brad ever again.

I'll never see Brad again.

I grit my teeth. If I'm going down, I'm going down fighting.

Two things happen in the next second that chuck all my plans out the window. The first is a long, loud screech that reverberates in the distance, and the second is the Zheng turning as one to face that direction.

Still holding my knives in a death grip, I turn around too.

Two more Zheng stride into view atop an old courthouse, pausing to puff out their chests and gaze down at us with piercing amber eyes. They raise their multiple tails high, mesmerizing us with another series of screeches that resonates through the streets. They're communicating with the Zheng around us, then they turn their glowing gaze towards me.

And I recognize them. The two Zheng from the earlier camp, the ones whose ironic humanity found their way into my heart.

The ones I freed.

That nagging, prickling feeling of being followed since we left that camp makes complete sense to me now.

With a final screech from the two Zheng on top of the building, all the other Zheng turn back to me and then to Sneery Glasses Guy.

They poise themselves to pounce on him.

'Oh my god,' the colour drains from Sneery Glasses Guy's face. 'I'm sorry . . . I'm sorry!' And just like that, his old snivelly self is back, the shifty eyes darting back and forth between the Zheng and me.

'Please don't let them kill me!' he gestures to the Zheng. 'There's more where they came from . . . and I'll tell you everything.'

14

Extra Life

When Qing Shan banks in a sudden dip, my stomach lurches. Then she spreads her wings wide and with a powerful whoosh, slices through the air at an upward angle. I screw my eyes shut and tighten my arms around her neck, the scales of her dragon hide iridescent against the night sky.

Below us and through the ruins of mankind, the Jiangshi vault over the rooftops of the buildings, a horde of Zheng in tow, because there's only the attack on Qing Feng Outpost in our minds now, with no more precautions as to wandering humans shooting us down. It's all disquiet and abandon and haste, snowballing into frayed nerves and ruptured resolves.

We've delayed our rescue long enough—I'm not even sure what the current state of the outpost is. Have the two Handlers managed to breach its defences and infiltrate the outpost, causing chaos and overpowering General Wu and his men? Have they defeated Siv despite her powerful horns, caught up with Connor, and . . . and—

I swallow.

Pietro and Izanami will head to the Zheng's lair with Sneery Glasses Guy. If he's looking for protection against the Ferals, Pietro—in his right state of mind—is more than enough to keep his refugees safe. He and Izanami will round up the rest of the

Zheng before anyone else tortures them, and hopefully restore them to the fold.

Which leaves me, Qing Shan, the Zheng from the camp and the Jiangshi as the only reinforcements for Connor; I can only pray that the Handlers haven't arrived—for now, that'll be enough.

When Qing Shan bares her fangs and screeches, every muscle in my body tenses. I grit my teeth in a vain attempt to convince myself I'm brave enough to handle whatever happens next.

Because we're here.

And we're too late.

As Qing Shan flaps her wings to gusts of wind on either side of me to brace for landing, I see it—Qing Feng Outpost in disarray, bodies strewn across the ground like ragdolls, blood splattered on the battleground like bursts of graffiti on an empty pavement. I immediately spot General Wu and his men leaping from one Feral to the next, working together to keep their blows synchronized and in relentless succession.

Qing Shan's claws plant themselves firmly on the ground and I leap off, the Jiangshi and the Zheng on either side of me springing into action. My adrenaline roars back to life. There's no time for strategy, no time to assess. Ignoring the pain from Sneery Glasses Guy's torture on my body, I grip my knives in each hand and charge.

Qing Shan rears up and claws at the face of a nearby Feral, and I slip down underneath it to slash two quick cuts on one of its legs. The Feral's deep growl directly overhead sounds like a sonic boom, and I slide out in the nick of time as it collapses to the ground. In the second before it recovers its footing, Qing Shan sinks her fangs onto its injured leg, flapping her wings to steer clear of the Feral's lethal horns. Struggling to regain its balance, the monster wails.

The blood singing in my ears galvanizes me into action. Weaving in and out between its wounded legs and its flailing tail,

I sneak quick stabs on its belly—one, two, three jabs—driving it over the edge into a berserk rage. It roars and kicks itself free from Qing Shan's bite.

It wobbles and finds its footing. Qing Shan and I brace ourselves as the Feral shrieks in wrath, unfurling its hideous tongue past its first row of fangs and its second inner mouth of humanoid teeth. It raises its horns into the sky but then stumbles back as two arrows from the distance plunge into its eyes with unerring aim.

I whip around. Siv is rushing towards us, her bow raised, and she lands three more blows onto the Feral's face, the third one landing straight into its gaping maw. It collapses, wailing, crying, and still so, so angry. When Qing Shan finds her opening, she lunges forward and claws at the three stab wounds I had inflicted on the Feral's belly, and a deluge of blood spills from its body. It twitches and rages and claws at the air, until, at long last, it stops moving.

I look down at my quivering fists, still gripping my two knives drenched in the Feral's blood.

One down—and so, so, so much more to go.

I bite down on my lip to muzzle the helplessness as Siv stands her ground in front of me, the havoc behind her a dystopia of loss.

She nods at me, her broken horn glistening red with what I hope isn't her blood. 'Glad to have you, luv.'

'Where's Connor?'

'Still trying to get that bloody beacon to work.' Siv's amber eyes do a quick sweep of the Jiangshi like she's looking for someone, likely a silver-haired, crimson-eyed leader who was with me when she saw me last. But she's gracious enough not to probe—instead, she gestures to the crumbling three-storeyed structure to our right. 'Go. We'll hold the fort here.'

I stare into her eyes and she stares right back like she understands.

'Thank you,' I tremble. With a final pat on Qing Shan's neck, I turn on my heel and rush into the building, leaving the chaos of the outside behind me.

Inside, the horror is palpable. Mangled wires fire sparks from the ceiling, crumbling walls spill their innards into the halls. The sharp scent of paint shooting up my nostrils actually buzzes my brain to life for a bit—this place must've been some kind of a paint shop before all this, but it's unrecognizable now, an overturned bucket here and a wayward pail there, flooding the walls and the floors with multicoloured splatters, like the building itself is already bleeding to death. There's nothing here now but the reality of the invasion, tainted with the slivered memories of what it once was.

'Connor?' I yell into the darkness, squinting as the occasional spark illuminates a spot here and there. I wade through the debris, doing my utmost to tune out the screeches outside, focusing instead on seeing those determined green eyes again through the haze.

'Connor?' I try one more time.

Nothing.

I crawl through a gap in a collapsed wall and emerge on the other side. The space looks very much like a meeting room with a long table down the middle and mangled office equipment against the walls. The gap I squeezed through is balanced precariously on some rubble—one wrong push will topple the entire roof. Pieces of what used to be chairs are strewn about, and there, curled on the floor beneath what used to be part of the ceiling, is a body.

'Connor?'

I call out again. This time, someone responds.

Or rather, *something*.

Two or three doors down and somewhere to my left, a low growl rumbles through the debris around me. It's not a screech, not a roar, not a Feral. It's the grunt of something more intelligent, more capable, something that has its wits about it and isn't a mindless, pressurized chunk of rage.

It's a Handler, somewhere down in the halls, and it's inside this building with me.

With us.

Shit. I scramble to the body on the ground and use my remaining strength to clear the debris, and it's an unconscious Connor, his face still etched with the same determination and agony that seared itself into my brain the day I left.

'Oh my god.' I feel for a pulse and my heart perks up for the first time in a long, long while.

He's alive, he's okay, and we need to get the hell out of here.

'Connor?' I whisper as another otherworldly grunt resonates through the halls around us. I scan his body for broken bones and any injuries and thank my luck stats that he doesn't seem to be hurt. A few more times of my whispering his name and he coughs, frowning up at me as the nightmare clicks back into place.

'Ava?' his eyes blink into focus as he tries to sit up. 'How—?'

'Yes, it's me—it's okay. You're okay,' I give in to a split second of weakness and hug him tight, grateful, so very grateful, that he's alive. 'We have to go.'

Connor coughs a few more times, then shakes his head. 'No.'

'No?' I help him to his feet and he leans against me until he finds his footing. 'There's a Handler here somewhere, Connor. If it finds us, we won't stand a chance.'

'We did it, Ava,' Connor focuses his gaze on me. 'We found a way to work through the beacon, and I have to send it to Leslie's contacts before it's too late.'

'What? You can't—'

'I was halfway through the transfer when something crashed through the building's wall.' He hobbles over to a nearby desk and true enough, a laptop is propped up on a chair to one side, flickering and holding on for dear life.

Connor hunches over the dying device and starts typing madly into it. 'I don't know how long the power will hold, or how long the Internet connection will last. I just need to send this over and we can go.'

Another grunt reverberates around us and my heart leaps to my throat. 'How long is it going to take?'

'I'm not sure,' Connor's eyes are rivetted to the screen. 'Two minutes tops?'

That's two minutes we don't have, I swallow, my eyes darting back and forth to see if there's some way we can barricade ourselves in. There isn't.

I grip my knives tighter and leave one on the table beside Connor. 'Whatever you need to do, do it quickly. I'll be right back.'

'What? Ava!' Connor whips around, but I'm already gone, sprinting down the hallway to my left. I grab one of the half-empty buckets of goop on the floor. If two minutes is what Connor needs to help save the world, two minutes is what I'm going to give him.

Somehow.

Throwing all rational thought out the window, I rush towards the grunting, which gets closer and closer through the fog of debris around me. I make no effort to stifle my breaths or muffle my footsteps, and just when I think the hallway can go no further, I skid to a stop.

The first thing I notice is its face. Cracked like it's been left out too long in the sun to dry in the worst possible way, its face is a map of angry ridges far more prominent than the ones on the Lightbringer's face, gnarled and protected by an exoskeleton. Black metal hulls cover the rest of the Handler, an impenetrable armour to keep that exoskeleton intact, a second layer of defence just in case the humans got too cocky or got any ideas.

The eight-foot monstrosity is hunched over in the cramped space of the hall, the building still too small to contain its massive frame despite the shattered walls. I instinctively know it's the same creature, that same Handler who was in charge of the initial wave of Ferals the mayor let loose during first contact, that very same Handler who's been looking for me because I blew up the Ferals' unhatched pods back then.

It's that same Handler who chased Brad and me through the woods that day, lopped off Brad's right leg, and shot him in the chest.

I fume.

The storm in me flushes out the fear, and it's all I need to keep going. I'm not exactly thinking clearly, and maybe in this situation, that's okay.

I need all the stupidity in the world to do what I'm about to do next.

'Hey, you!' I wave my arms in big gestures just in case it hasn't noticed me yet, but it has—it's been staring back at me for as long as I've been staring at it, and it is so, so pissed.

The cracked eyebrows knit together and another explosive grunt almost cleaves the floor beneath me. When I'm sure I've held its attention long enough, I hurl the bucket I've been lugging around straight at its face.

The thick, dark-coloured liquid explodes on the Handler's visor, hopefully obstructing its vision long enough to save my life. As soon as it roars in my general direction, I dash to my right after my little taunt—and it works.

The Handler stomps after me, every step causing tremors on the ground I'm standing on. My mind flits to the structural integrity of this building for a second before I focus on the task at hand—an enraged Handler chasing after me in an enclosed space within the cramped building with no clear way out. And all I have to do is keep this up for two minutes.

Two minutes.

Two minutes for Connor to send out his message, and two minutes for me to stay alive.

The Handler calls and it almost sounds like it's right behind my ear, but I don't trust myself to look over my shoulder at the rashness of what I've done. I turn the next corner, and the next corner, and the next, trying to map out the same path I had navigated when I was looking for Connor.

Finally, finally, I circle back to the room where I found Connor and thank the RNG gods that he looks up at me just in time.

'Two minutes,' I pant, and he nods.

'Let's go.'

I lead him to the crevice that I crawled through when I found him, when a growl rolls down the hall to our left. Connor freezes. 'What was that?'

'We have to go. *Now*,' I shove him in the direction of the gap, and as he squeezes through, I keep an eye on the tiny rocks crumbling with every shimmy he makes. As soon as he makes it out to the other side, he reaches for me through the crack.

Just as another grunt rages from the hallway and I turn.

The Handler pauses at the other end of the hall, just a few feet from where I am. It says something in a garbled language I can't understand, and it charges.

It *charges*.

'Ava!' Connor yells from the other side. I don't need telling twice.

I duck and launch myself through the hole in the wall. The Handler's footsteps thunder closer, splitting the already fragmented debris around the hole. I clench my jaw and scramble as fast as I can through the tightening crater and a sharp pain snags at my side. I know I've cut my stomach somewhere, somehow, but I can't afford to dwell on this now. Connor tugs me to the other side just as something swipes at the air right where my feet used to be and it's the Handler, and it's livid, and it's right here and it breaches through the crevice.

Connor and I dive to the floor. The Handler, for all its strength and anger and heavy, heavy armour, bursts halfway through the wall and then the ceiling comes crashing down.

The entire upper floor collapses. The image of the Handler's cracked face seething with fury brands itself into my mind's eye. It roars at me just before the whole building caves in.

Which means Connor and I have seconds before we're buried alive.

We scramble to our feet and make a mad dash to the front door as everything falls apart around us, and just when I think we've made it out alive and the harsh night breeze hits our face, we barely have time to breathe when a deafening *boom* behind us makes us turn back around in horror.

It's the Handler, and it's here, and it's alive. The whole building imploding on it didn't do squat.

Connor and I brace ourselves with one knife each for all the good they'll do. Behind us, the chaos of the Ferals and our friends rages on, and in front of us, a Handler stands.

The relief of surrender washes over me when Connor clasps his hand over mine beside him. *We did what we could*, he seems to say. *We did what we could.*

He breathes my name and I breathe his right back, and this is it, there's no more awkwardness or high-school crushes or petty online tournaments. All those sundaes I've ever had at Marcello's are the last I'll ever have. I'll never learn the secret recipe to Aunt Steph's chicken sandwiches and I'll never know Big Bad Wolf's real name. I won't see Jimmy or Ethan or Harley ever again, and I'll never go on a tour of Luna's hometown or discover the Minokawa with her like she promised.

I'll never know if humanity can survive this attack, if the world will ever be the same again or if we'll ever recover from the scars of the past. And eventually, even the brightest light will blink out in time; it'll fade away, snuffed out and insignificant, that not even its memory will make sense to anyone or anything at all.

The Handler roars.

I stand my ground as bile bubbles up my stomach. My heart shoots up to take a chokehold of my throat. My tears triumph, finally crying for me.

It takes one step towards me and Connor.

But then.

Something knocks the Handler over with a force that shakes the ground.

It falls.

Something pries the melee weapon from the Handler's hands in an instant. Now, unarmed and on the ground, the Handler roars at its assailant, who is moving so fast that I have to focus hard to see whom the alien is fighting against.

I almost don't recognize Brad with this livid, almost feral look in his fiery eyes. He leaps onto the Handler's body and sinks his knees onto its chest, denting its armour with the impact alone. The Handler struggles to get up but Brad counters with a punch every split second, the Handler growling and Brad screeching as he pummels fist after fist onto the Handler's helmet until the glass or whatever it is shatters.

He doesn't let up.

Brad flexes his fingers now and claws at the Handler's cracked face in a frenzy, his fangs bared and his face twisted into something I don't recognize—something alien. It doesn't take long before dark, almost black, liquid squirts from the Handler's face. I watch in horror as its body slowly, slowly stops writhing. Its roars grow fainter and die out altogether.

Brad doesn't stop.

Streaks of red have started to splatter against his fists now and spread up his arms, mixing with the dark liquid that oozes out of the Handler's face. The eerie image of Brad kneeling atop the creature as he claws deeper and deeper with his fingers into its unmoving face immobilizes me, until Connor releases my hand.

'Brad,' he calls out. 'Brad!'

Brad snaps out of his manic trance, and he sits there, his whole body shaking.

'That's enough, man,' Connor says. 'That's enough.'

I realize my tears haven't stopped falling since the Handler made a move towards us a moment ago, and now, when Brad turns towards us, I see that his face is streaked with tears too.

But there's something else in Brad's face now, and it's not just the specks of the Handler's blood mushrooming all over his skin. There's despair in there, and wrath, at himself and at the world for whatever reason. My heart goes out to him.

What has he done? What happened with the Lightbringer back in the cave? What is Brad to me now, and what has he become?

His eyes search mine somehow, the loneliness and the desperation in there somewhere, searching for forgiveness or pity or…I don't even know anymore.

And as I watch him and his trembling form, still on top of the Handler like he's just won but he hasn't, I think to myself that this is the reality of war, the necessity of victory. Is this the price of him owning up to his title as the Harbinger? Is this what it takes to shepherd his people?

Is this the cost of leadership?

Does it cost you your humanity?

As the agony of the truth crashes down on me, the pain in my side rushes back with a vengeance, my adrenaline depleted. I look down at my trembling hand and realize I've been clutching my side this whole time, and it's now blackened with blood.

Mine. My side. Something I snagged when I crawled through the gap in the wall.

The sting of copper shoots up my nostrils and everything feels faint. My vision blurs. My legs give way.

The last thing I hear is Connor shouting my name and Brad leaping off the Handler and maybe this is it, this is how it ends.

I close my eyes and give in, a faint melody of sadness wrapping itself around my heart.

It's a lonely lullaby, and it's singing about everything we've lost.

15

Continue?

Something rocks under me. I feel like clawing into the air, but I realize just how tired I am—almost a plea for release. A gentle hand strokes my hair in slow, tentative caresses.

Everything else comes alive in waves. I'm lying on something that sways from side to side with a constant yet unpredictable motion. Pain sears my side and with every breath I take, it feels like something's piercing my stomach from the inside.

The voices come next—strange yet familiar disembodied voices, drifting in and out of focus all around me.

'They keep disappearing without a trace because there *aren't* any traces to look for.'

'Is it all underground?'

'Every single thing. A personal workforce, coerced into building his tech against their will.'

'That's . . . a lot to take in. You okay there, Brad?'

The gentle hand on my hair stops stroking and a low, guttural voice rumbles from above me, 'I will be.' He sighs, and my head moves with his body. 'I should be.'

At this, I force my eyes open, but even that proves to be a struggle.

'Ava?' Brad's whisper hovers above me. I lift my lids as slowly as I can, the glare of sunlight making me squint. 'You're awake. Thank the heavens . . .'

My vision morphs into focus, and the first thing I see is Brad's bloodied face just inches above mine. For a second my heart constricts, because with the mix of alien blood still caked to his face and the dried trail of liquid trickling down his ruby eyes and staining his pale skin, Brad looks . . .

. . . terrifying.

He shifts his body and I realize that we're all on a small boat of sorts; I'm on my back with my head pillowed on Brad's lap, his hand on my forehead. Captain Yongliang is standing over us both with a worried look in his eyes, along with a few Jiangshi, a handful of Zheng, some of Leslie's tech team, Siv and Connor.

Connor's still here.

'Hey,' Connor sits down beside Brad and leans over at me. 'Took you long enough.'

That remark tugs at the corner of my lips, and I almost feel like smiling.

Almost.

I try to sit up and Brad immediately supports my torso with one arm, wrapping his other arm around my shoulders. The moment I sit up and lean my body against him, I wince.

'I'm sorry, Ava,' he breathes, laying a hand on my side. I look down. A makeshift bandage is haphazardly fastened around my waist, stained pink with what can only be my own blood. 'I never should've left your side, especially since I promised to keep you safe.'

He bows his head at Connor then, who waves a bandaged hand.

'Hey man, we all make mistakes.' Connor shakes his head. 'It's only human.'

Connor's statement takes Brad aback, and I watch as his eyes go from surprise to gratitude to guilt. Brad once told me that he has never quite felt like he truly belonged, and that it's the most disquieting thing not knowing how to fit in. This is probably one of the few times anyone's actually regarded him as human.

But the thing is, I'm not really sure what it means to be human these days—not anymore.

'What—' I cough out and immediately regret it. My injured side feels like it's on fire. 'What happened?'

'We got rid of the remaining Handler and his Ferals at Qing Feng Outpost, luv,' Siv cocks her head, beaming at me like everything was just fine and dandy. I notice that her other horn is also damaged now, giving her an uneven, jagged, unhinged look. 'Connor made the right call.'

Connor flinches. 'I . . . there was . . . someone else trapped inside the building when it collapsed. I thought I heard someone scream . . . and I wanted to find whoever that was after things settled down. But we had to leave before more Ferals arrived, so . . .' He looks down. 'There . . . there was nothing left to save, anyway.'

Siv nods at Connor's justification of his actions, and the air suddenly feels thick with shame. 'The important thing is that the information got through to Leslie's contacts. We can only hope they know what to do with it.'

Two massive shadows hover overhead and I look up to see Zahir and Qing Shan flapping their wings in unison. I strain my neck to peer over the side of the boat at the vast expanse of blue all around us, and notice silhouettes slithering beneath the surface on either side of the boat. The outlines of what look like humans with massive fish tails speed along beside us towards . . . wherever the heck we're going.

I turn back to Brad and manage to croak out my next words. 'The Lightbringer?'

At this, Brad clenches his jaw and scowls, making his bloodied face look even eerier. 'He revealed his true colours to me. It's clear where his loyalties lie now.'

'It was him,' a Jiangshi with rows of badges pinned on his chest butts in with a sombre expression on his face. I finally get to see General Wu up close. 'For the longest time, we always wondered how the Hostiles found us here, how they knew exactly what to do and exactly where to look. The answer turned out to be pretty simple: they had inside help.'

'Those magnetized blades grazed me once,' Siv raises her right arm and shows me three flesh wounds on her triceps, the gashes still livid and scarred despite their healing ability. 'The Hostiles knew exactly how to disable us and keep us from Binding again, and now we know why.'

My breath catches.

The only person who knew about all the ins and outs of the Binding was the only one who could've used that knowledge against the Pure.

The Lightbringer. Of course.

He has led both hope and ruin for the Pure here. This was exactly what the Jinmenju warned us about.

'He Binded with a Hostile and that ordeal drove him mad,' Brad clenches his fist. 'For whatever reason, he brought the Hostiles here. I'm going to kill him myself.'

Rage emanates from Brad's body, regret and sorrow and so many questions all balled up inside with it. He has fully owned his role now as the Harbinger, the only one who can lead his people to victory.

But why does it still feel like something's wrong?

The uncomfortable truth dawns upon our little group. Failure waves its mercy over us, and as if on cue, something opens up in the distance, breaking the monotony of the endless stretch of blue.

Over the horizon, the shore comes into view as we speed towards land. But the sight that greets us along the shoreline sinks my heart.

Lined up along the beach are hordes and hordes of Hostiles, all armoured up on top of their exoskeletons, armed with some form of weapon in each of their hands. They seem smaller and swifter than the Handlers we've encountered—likely footsoldiers and warriors to the very core. There are no longer any Ferals in sight—no more mindless dogs let loose only to cause mayhem and panic among the inferior beings they want to conquer.

Now, these Hostiles are smarter, more skilled, and more efficient, and finally, finally, the real invasion has begun.

I find myself holding Brad's hand with one hand and Connor's with the other, and they both squeeze mine back, Brad with the blood on his face and Connor with the reality of what he had to leave behind.

Sneery Glasses Guy was right.

We need monsters to fight monsters, and I can't help but feel like that's exactly what we've all become.

* * *

Acknowledgements

Is it still worth it if it costs you your humanity? Saving the world against so-called monsters isn't easy, and I wanted to make sure Ava knew the consequences—it's not all fun and games, after all. Book One was like the honeymoon phase, but in Book Two, the excitement of stepping into a whole new world begins to fade, and Ava starts to see the crises people face and the lies we tell ourselves to survive along the way.

Much like Ava's struggles, I had plenty of my own while crafting this story, which is why once again, my eternal gratitude goes to my beta readers and fab friends, K.B. Meniado and Honey Mabalot, who never fail to squeal and lament with me as they chip away at the edges of my stories to shape them into what they are today; to Stephanie Sia, who reads every single word of all my WIPs and who will forever hate me for conjuring Connor into existence; to the ever-amazing Bryce Allen King, my go-to legal expert, who's always happy to scrutinize my contracts (and to whom I owe an entire paragraph).

Thank you to the beautiful souls and overall lovely human beings at Penguin Random House SEA: Thatchaa, whose love and passion for my work shine through with every single edit she makes, without whom my MS wouldn't be what it is; Garima, whose enthusiasm and efforts always make me feel incredibly honoured for her time; Alkesh, Ishani, Rupal, Pallavi and Chai for their relentless support and incredible patience; superwoman

Nora, who tirelessly champions our works day and night by giving our stories a home (I don't think she ever sleeps).

My heartfelt appreciation goes to my fellow Penguin novelists for being the most fabulous support group: Marga Ortigas, Danton Remoto, Daryl Kho. And of course, these incredible women: Kayce Teo, Joyce Chua, and Eva Wong Nava—being part of the 'Scribe Tribe' with these master wordsmiths is a true honour and I will forever be grateful for their love, laughter, tears, silliness, wisdom and friendship.

To my family: my parents, who always show up to all my events and gave me access to all the books as a kid; my brother, who knows my own voice and style like the back of his hand; my husband, whose ideas need to be reined in and translated into my words because he's just that creative—thank you all from the bottom of my heart.

To my closest friends and my #romanceclass and BRUMultiverse family, thank you for going through this author life together.

Of course, as always, none of this would be possible without the Big Guy up there.

The *Of Myths and Men* trilogy is pure escapism, and I hope you've felt the same throughout your journey with Ava and her mythical friends. Thank you, dearest reader, for sticking by her as she grapples with monsters both inner and outer here—hopefully, you'll still be along for the ride as she journeys to the conclusion of her story in the next book. Until then, I hope that, like Ava, you've learned to find friends in the unlikeliest of places, but also found the strength to value the existing ones that are worth keeping.

Thank you for pressing START to save the world—now, let's hit that CONTINUE button, shall we?